Five Children
and a Dog

The five children depended on Turi. He was their best friend and the only family Giangi and Rags really had. What would they do now that Turi had won a music scholarship to Milan? It seemed only natural to the children to follow him.

Turi was touched when he found them on the train, but how would he take care of them? Giangi the youngest was five and Antonio the oldest was only thirteen. Life in the huge, cold city would be tough after their warm and sunny Sicilian island.

How the children managed to get along using their ingenuity and determination involved them in some intriguing and often amusing adventures.

Renée Reggiani's writing vibrates with a true Italian flavor and liveliness. Her awareness of people and her understanding of life make this a perceptive as well as entertaining, vital adventure.

FIVE CHILDREN
AND A DOG

by Renée Reggiani

illustrated by Margot Tomes

Translated from the Italian by
Mary Lambert and Anne Chisholm

Coward-McCann, Inc.   New York

This book was first published under the title
"Le Avventure di cinque ragazzi e un cane"

First American Edition
© 1960 Renée Reggiani
© 1964, 1965 Renée Reggiani

Library of Congress Catalog Card Number: 65-13285
MANUFACTURED IN THE UNITED STATES OF AMERICA
102014
Second Impression

To Mother Olga

CONTENTS

Part One

Part Two

Contents

Part Three

FIVE CHILDREN
AND A DOG

Part
One

Turi and the Band

GIANGI CAME running down the dusty footpath with Tom at his heels. He was late.

The country all around was far too tempting; how could a boy of five be expected to resist? He was full to bursting with figs, and so were his pockets. They were someone else's, of course, but they had been so deliciously sweet and juicy that he could still taste them as he ran. Even now some were turning sticky in his pockets.

Tom had been in on the raid too, but being a poodle, he had not really liked the bitter taste of the green skin. In fact he shook his head over it and spit it out. But, after all, he *was* an animal.

He was, however, the nicest possible kind of animal. Tom was a special dog, a highly intelligent dog. He was the most special of all the dogs in the world, and the most special poodle there has ever been. For one thing, he could talk. That is, he talked to Giangi, for they understood each other perfectly.

Giangi then, with his faithful Tom, came running down the path. He was late for an important meeting.

When he arrived at the gate of the little garden—it was really no more than a bare patch surrounded by a spindly myrtle hedge, with only one tree to give a bit of shade—he was greeted by the sound of a small orchestra.

Oh, how late we are! thought Giangi and Tom together, as they squeezed between the hedge and the gate as unobtrusively as possible. They wriggled stealthily in.

Of course, they did not get away with it.

Rosalia glared at them and rattled her tambourine; Antonio shook his head reprovingly and opened his accordion full blast—far wider than was really necessary. And Giuseppangelo, nicknamed Tufty because of his hair, which stood straight up on end, sneezed with delight, winked at them and strummed a few welcoming notes on his guitar. The latecomers had arrived; even a blind man would have known that.

Being late was not what mattered. Nobody would punish Giangi, or make him go without his supper. (Anyway, he had already had the figs for supper, and

there were often days when he had to make do with less.) No, it was purely a question of self-respect. What Giangi really minded was the disappointed glance Turi gave him as he looked up for a moment from his clarinet. This hurt far more than a thousand reproaches or a good beating.

Who was Turi, anyway?

A great speech could be made about him, but two or three words will do. Turi was a really good man. Just that. An extra-specially good man. When he was a child he had suddenly found himself alone in the world. It had been one of those tragedies which so often seem to happen to the nicest and most defenseless people. He had been too young at the time to wonder much why and how it had happened—and he still hadn't really found out.

He had sat and cried for a little on the steps of a church. Then he had had to concentrate on getting enough to eat. It was hard at first, and he often had to go hungry, but he managed.

Giangi was like a son to him. One day, after the war was over for that particular part of Sicily, Turi came upon the little boy, lost and in tears, sitting forlornly on some church steps. It was a strange coincidence, and the sight of the small orphan must have reminded Turi vividly of his own sad childhood.

Giangi's father was an engineer from the North who

had come to work on the island, but he and his wife were both killed in a machine-gun attack. Their little boy somehow escaped unhurt, and crept away to the church where Turi found him, crying with fright, exhausted and hungry.

Turi did not hesitate. Without a word he took Giangi's hand and led him home. It was really only a hut, but better than nothing. From then on everything that Turi had must do for two. And that was that.

Nobody ever knew if Giangi had other relatives in the North; he was too young to remember anything much, or to explain. And so he stayed with Turi, and no one ever came to look for him.

Turi was like a father to Giangi, and even more. He was someone who had rescued him as if by magic, at the most terrible moment of his life. When everything was black and terrifying, Turi had suddenly appeared and given him food and shelter. Above all, what meant most to Giangi was that here was someone, a real person, to whom he mattered, who understood him and who knew how to talk to him.

Turi worked for the local farmers. They in their turn worked for the landowners who owned groves of olives and oranges. The dry ground was full of stones and one of Turi's jobs was to collect them. First he put them in piles, then he built them into mile after mile of little walls. It was a thankless task, and the work

was as heavy and hard as the stones themselves. Turi's wages were often not money but a little olive oil, a few tomatoes or perhaps some olives. Whatever it was, he was glad to have it, especially now that he had Giangi to feed as well. At first Giangi was very pale and weak, but Turi, to his immense pride and delight, soon succeeded in making a healthy little boy of him.

Turi also did odd jobs as a carpenter, and one way or another he managed to make ends meet. Once the war was over, the local authorities did not hesitate long before allowing him to keep the boy. At first they simply could not believe that Giangi had arrived out of nowhere, but their few efforts to trace his family were fruitless, and anyway they soon came to realize that he and Turi belonged together.

Apart from Giangi, Turi's great love, his main interest and the most important thing in his life was music.

Why was this? Where did this great passion come from? Who knows? Perhaps long ago one of his ancestors had played a reed pipe as he led his flocks over the bare hillside, or as he wandered home along the seashore after a day's fishing.

Turi's greatest ambition was to have his own band. He would dream of this all through the long summer evenings, when the heat brought people to their doorways to look up at the countless bright stars of the Sicilian sky, and he thought about it during the long

15

day's work in the fields and as he carried loads of olives to the press.

But it was only a lovely dream, as unattainable as one of the thousand stars in the sky above. They looked so very near, as if he need only reach up his hand to touch them, and yet they were hopelessly, impossibly far away.

But Turi was full of ideas and did not give up easily. He started his own band, with four children whom he trained himself. They practiced with him every day in his small garden.

CHAPTER TWO

Tufty's Brainstorm

IT HAD NOT BEEN at all easy for Turi to get the band together.

First of all he had to find children in the neighborhood who really cared enough about music to devote themselves completely to making this dream come true. Then they had to be prepared to put up with quarrels and even beatings from their families, who of course wanted nothing to do with such goings-on.

Finally they had to find the money to buy their instruments. This was the real problem. Money. It was just a word, but how could they ever get hold of enough? They didn't dare even to think about the actual money but concentrated on schemes for raising it.

Tufty was the first to hit on a way. He had such a brilliant plan that the others were speechless with admiration.

Giuseppangelo Baroni, nicknamed Tufty, was the
tenth child of an enormous family which for genera-
tions had worked for the local landowners. His father
and his older brothers worked long hours on the es-
tates of a rich and noble family who lived in a magnificent palace in the great city of Palermo.

Every so often, a surveyor, called Giuseppangelo
Castronuovo, would come to Marzamemi to survey the
surrounding lands. Devoted as this good man was to
the land, his schemes for irrigation and other improve-
ments never got any farther than his notebooks. Although there seemed little point in it, Castronuovo
continued to plan and slave away; the work was as
much a part of him as his daily bread. He would often
stop on his rounds to chat with the farmers, and
though his talk was usually above their heads, he
would air his views on life and work, and comment
sadly on the many things men plan but somehow
never carry out.

He would joke good-naturedly with old Baroni, and
tease him about his large family. But he always took
a real interest in how things were going.

One day Baroni asked him, "Would your honor consider becoming godfather to my last son?"

"Will he really be your last?" Castronuovo grinned.
He could well have done without the title "Your
Honor," but it would keep slipping into Baroni's con-
versation—his people had used it for longer than they

could remember. The surveyor was testing an orange between his fingers as he spoke. Another of his businesses was selling oranges, both on the mainland and abroad, so he knew a lot about them. He was an able man, broad-minded, good at his job, and indeed at whatever he turned his hand to. Anyway he said "yes" to Baroni, and this was how Tufty came to have such a kind godfather, although of course he didn't know about it at the time. He was given a medallion on a real gold chain to wear around his neck. Every so often he would write a short note to his godfather at his father's dictation, and send it off to Palermo. Soon afterward back would come another little present.

This was Tufty's plan: why not write his very own letter to his godfather?

Tufty did well at school. His father had decided, partly because he had indeed turned out to be the last son and partly because he had such a well-educated godfather, to make a big effort and send him to the high school at Syracuse.

My respected godfather, this comes to bring you my respectful greetings and to let you know that I am in good health and hope that you and your family are likewise.

Guiseppangelo Castronuovo was completely alone in the world, and so it is not quite clear for whom this last phrase was intended.

I have done well at school and have moved up into

the second class, as you wished. I hoped that you would be pleased and perhaps send me a present as you do every year . . . Tufty put down his pen and scratched his untidy head. Something about that sentence bothered him, but he could not decide quite what. Never mind, this letter to his godfather had to be written at all costs, even if it didn't turn out perfectly. The main thing was to make his godfather realize that the request was terribly important. After all, he had never before asked for anything more than news of his godfather's health.

. . . and what I should really like is a guitar.

But it must not be just a toy. It had to be a real guitar, with strings—one he could really play.

One that I can really play, he added after a moment's thought.

With very best wishes, your devoted godson, Giuseppangelo Baroni.

The letter stopped a little abruptly after the guitar bit, but then that was the bit that mattered. At least he had not put "I kiss your honor's hand," as his father always wanted him to, because . . . well, why? Why should he have to write that he kissed someone's hand when he never ever did?

Just where Giuseppangelo managed to scrounge a stamp remains a mystery to this day. But the fact is that the letter went through the mail, reached Signor

Castronuovo at Palermo and not long afterwards a registered parcel arrived addressed to Tufty. Inside there was a magnificent guitar, with colored ribbons knotted around the neck. A real guitar. One he could really play.

The first instrument for Turi's orchestra had been found.

Words cannot describe Tufty's face when he saw the new guitar. His dream had come true. There in front of him was a guitar. That sort of thing doesn't happen every day. Tufty stared at it, stroked the glossy wood, the smooth curves and the long graceful neck with its bright dangling ribbons. Some time passed before he could bring himself to try the new instrument.

It was soon clear that Tufty had talent.

Turi declared this to be so. He played his clarinet in the same way, almost by instinct. Admittedly the old bandmaster at Noto had taught him a little basic musical theory, but then the bandmaster had been dead for years now.

The second one to appear with an instrument was Rosalia.

Rosalia Ruggero's family had handed down from father to son a passion for singing to the tambourine. This time it had gone from father to daughter, and Rosalia received from her grandfather's hands the ancient family tambourine, its wooden circle all inlaid with little metal disks. If Giuseppangelo was proud of his shining guitar, Rosalia was no less proud of her tambourine. It was so old and venerable and full of tradition. There were so many drawings and colored patterns and names inscribed on the frame, and on both sides of the skin, that there was room for nothing more.

Rosalia was especially lucky because her family was on her side. Far from being annoyed, they could not have been more pleased with her.

For the others things were much more complicated. Tufty was given such a horrible beating that it could well have made him lose all desire to play the guitar for the rest of his life. His father was furious with him over the secret negotiations with his godfather and his impudence in asking for such a big present. What was the use of it anyway?

Tufty crept away to a secret hiding place and cried and cried over the new guitar—being very careful not to wet the strings—and then began to stroke it again and, after a while, he managed a smile. He sat there under the old olive tree overlooking the sea, leaning against the great scar in its trunk, which was smooth and barkless and the color of scorched earth. It was there that he tried to play his first few chords on the guitar. He felt a thrill of pure joy such as he had never

known in all his eleven years. All at once he hardly knew whether his hesitant fingers on the strings made those sounds, or the gentle breeze stirring the leaves of the olive tree, showing them green on one side, silver on the other.

The wind stirred the leaves on the olive trees. He, Tufty, had fingers which could play the guitar. This was something wonderful. A discovery indeed.

CHAPTER THREE

Antonio's Idea

ANTONIO HAD the hardest task of all.

An accordion is an extremely expensive thing, and although Antonio had already started working and was earning money, he had to hand over every penny to help support his family.

Antonio Messina was a tall, strong boy, and very thoughtful for his thirteen years. An unruly lock of soft fair hair was always falling across his forehead. He had a wide, honest face and bright blue eyes. (Not all Sicilians are dark, for some have Nordic ancestors.)

Antonio's idea came to him one market day in Noto.

The market was held in a narrow, sloping street, flanked on one side by houses and on the other by the high, grim walls of the prison.

The prisoners sold things, too. At the entrance gate

there was always a display of straw and wickerwork seats, small couches and easy chairs, and wastepaper baskets that the prisoners had woven. Antonio could never see all this without feeling a slight pang. He could not bear to think that outside all was sunshine and happiness, with jostling crowds, the cries of the traders, children chewing nougat and blowing whistles with gay red balloons dancing over their heads, while inside there were men shut up behind boarded windows listening to the shouts and the bustle.

Not even the tortures inflicted by Attila the Hun— one of the few things he remembered learning about in school—could have been worse.

"Antonio! Antonio!" His mother was buying an earthenware jug, the kind that is so good for carrying water to the fields and keeping it cool while you work. She wanted some soup bowls too, but they were rather expensive and she had not quite made up her mind.

With Antonio carrying the jug, he and his mother elbowed and jostled their way through the market and finally, after many calculations on their fingers, they bought four earthenware soup bowls crudely decorated with green and pale brown stripes.

Antonio was vaguely aware that several craftsmen in the district made these pieces of pottery, and either sold them to the stall holders or came to the market to sell them themselves.

Suddenly Antonio had his brainstorm. Why shouldn't he make pottery, too? It would be a way of earning money toward buying his accordion.

Heaven knows why Antonio had set his heart on an accordion. It seemed somehow an important instrument, what with all those shining buttons down one side and the bellows which opened like a yawning red throat on the other. Anyway, to Antonio it represented the sum total of utter bliss—and perhaps he was not far wrong.

But how could he learn the secrets of making pottery, which in the end, he felt sure, would lead him to the secrets of playing the accordion?

On a sudden impulse, but first making sure his mother was some way off, Antonio asked a little hunchback with a kindly face whether he happened to know of anyone who made this earthenware pottery.

"Why, indeed I do," replied the hunchback smiling. "Myself for one."

Antonio was taken aback. He reddened and hesitated. "*You* do?"

"Yes, me. I do."

"Oh."

Antonio picked up a small, strangely colored clay figure of a woman. He looked at it. There was a little spout sticking out of its back. It was a whistle.

"Do you like it?" the hunchback asked.

"Oh, yes," Antonio said, "but I'm grown-up now. I don't play with toys anymore. Where do you live?"

"In Floridia. I'm the village baker, but when I'm not kneading dough I knead clay to make pottery."

"I'd love to watch you," murmured Antonio, almost to himself.

"Well then, come and visit me," the hunchback said warmly. "Ask in Floridia for Orestes the baker. Everyone knows me."

"Oh, thank you," Antonio replied and hurried off to find his mother.

It was not easy for Antonio to find an excuse to go to Floridia. Besides working in the vineyards, Antonio's father had a fishing boat for which he had saved for years. When he had a good catch he would pack his fish tightly in wooden crates and go and sell them in Syracuse.

He would load the crates onto his donkey cart and set off. Sicilian donkeys are small, shaggy, stouthearted and strong. The carts they pull are not always as brightly painted as they look in pictures, but they are strong and serviceable.

Antonio's father had one of these carts. It was quite a pretty one, although the paint needed touching up where it had been faded by rain and by seawater dripping from the fish crates. And it was on this cart, one morning after a good night's fishing, that he loaded the crates all ready for a trip to Syracuse.

Antonio leaped onto the cart and seized the reins. "Papa, *I'll* go today!"

"Nonsense! You don't know how to sell fish!"

"Oh yes I do!"

"No!"

"Yes!"

No, yes, the argument became heated. "Very well then, go," his father said at last. Antonio didn't need to be told twice. He gave such a jerk to the reins and such a crack of the whip that Rinaldo—the donkey—literally hurled himself forward, so violently in fact that all the crates swayed and tottered, and several mullet, less resigned to their fate than the others, almost escaped.

"Take care!" his father called after him. But Antonio did not hear.

He was happy.

He was off—on his way at last to making his greatest dream come true, even if he still had a long way to go. And all through his own doing. He felt light as air and ready to face anything.

"Rinaldo!" he cried, cracking the whip. Rinaldo pricked up his shaggy ears. Rinaldo was the name of a great knight whose deeds Antonio knew by heart, as all true Sicilians do. The donkey must have been proud to bear such a name.

"Do you realize that we are going to Floridia to-day?" Rinaldo jogged along as fast as he could. "Are

you listening, Rinaldo? Today we're free. We're going to see the hunchback." Rinaldo flapped his ears to show that he understood the importance of the expedition.

"Rinaldo! Rinaldo! Fight with Ferrau, to win your Angelica fair! Clash, clash, clash. (Sound of swords)," recited Antonio at the top of his voice. Rinaldo was tremendously excited and nearly broke into a trot, which was almost unheard-of for him.

Antonio began imagining. . . . Ferrau could stand for his own lack of money, Angelica for the accordion for which he had to fight, and he, Antonio, would be Rinaldo, the proud knight and follower of Charlemagne. The best stories, even the most farfetched, always ring true.

If it had not been for his accordion, Antonio would secretly have liked to become a storyteller, like those he had listened to in the village square at Noto, and in Marzamemi, his own village.

They would set up a sort of trestle on the ground, unroll the first sheet of pictures and hang it up, then sit on a chair or stool and begin to tell their story. Each picture showed a different scene from the same tale.

> "When Charlemagne, that happy king,
> Sat upon a golden throne
> His knights around him in a ring . . ."

Antonio knew many of these stories, and could have told them almost as well as the storytellers themselves.

Picture No. 1. King Charlemagne seated at the round table, surrounded by the gallant knights of France and the most famous warriors of the day, including the Saracens.

Picture No. 2. The appearance of Angelica, the beautiful young maiden, "fair as the morning star," followed by four giants and a knight, her brother.

Picture No. 3. All the knights, including Orlando, fall in love with Angelica, the daughter of the king of Cathay. Ferrau kills her brother Argalia in a fierce duel. Clash, Clash, Clash. (Sound of swords.)

Picture No. 4. In a wood. Angelica flees, pursued by Orlando and Rinaldo.

Look out for the traffic lights! Clever Rinaldo—the donkey, of course—had stopped at the first set of traffic lights in Syracuse, right at the entrance to the town. *He* wasn't dreaming of Angelica, but of a nice bunch of hay garnished with a few choice thistle tops.

Just before the bridge, Antonio touched the reins and turned off to the left. He pulled up outside the Bandiera Restaurant, and his friend Carlo appeared in the doorway.

Suddenly a crowd of small children about six or seven years old appeared from nowhere and swarmed around Rinaldo and the cart, pestering for something to eat. They wouldn't go away. It was a holiday and they had nothing better to do. Whenever anything interesting happened, a slight traffic jam or anything at all out of the ordinary, a swarm of dirty, ragged children would appear in a flash, pushing and shoving and yelling, simply for the fun of it.

"Will you buy my fish?" asked Antonio. Carlo nodded, tilting his chin and eying him keenly; there was something almost Oriental about his dark, slanting eyes.

"How much?"

"I always give the fair price," the young man answered.

"Fine. Let's unload. Clear out, all of you." The urchins shouted more than ever and hopped about all over the place—the soles of their feet were black. They did not, however, go away.

Carlo and Antonio carried the boxes into the huge and spotless kitchen. Water was boiling for spaghetti and the tomato sauce was simmering in a pan.

The transaction was soon over and they said good-bye.

Instead of going straight back to Marzamemi, Antonio took a turn off to the right and headed for Floridia. At Floridia someone showed Antonio where to find the hunchback's bakery.

Orestes was only just able to see over his own counter. At this time of day he was busy selling bread and the shop was full of people, but as soon as Antonio came in Orestes recognized him and seemed pleased to see him.

To one side, rows of new loaves were standing on long wooden tables waiting for the dough to rise. They were pale and puffy, and still soft under the light crusts that were just beginning to form. In the back of the shop a great square oven was roaring away.

"Today I make enough bread for the whole week," Orestes explained, coming over to Antonio when he had finished serving his customers. He left the counter in the charge of a hungry-looking boy, whose only food was probably the bread Orestes gave him, with an occasional raw tomato when he was in luck. He took Antonio into a room adjoining the shop. Here too there was an oven, but a smaller one; and here too there was work in progress. But it was with clay, not dough; and the molds needed to dry, not rise.

"First I knead in there, and then I knead in here," said the hunchback proudly. "And that's how I make my living."

His wretched hump gave extra meaning to what he said; he had worked hard, and his interest and enthusiasm had helped him forget his deformity.

Orestes went over to a wooden bench and uncovered a sort of shapeless mound covered with a damp rag. "You must remember always to keep it damp. This is the clay that pottery is made from." He took a lump of the clay and began to work it with his fingers with such enjoyment that it was a pleasure to watch him and Antonio longed to try for himself.

"And where do I get some?" he asked.

"I can get some for you. Don't worry about that."

One problem solved, thought Antonio. But the trickiest was still to come.

Orestes worked away at the clay. Gradually Antonio began to see two legs, arms, a helmet, a shield—and there was a small statue of an ancient warrior, perfect in every detail.

"And here you have Orestes himself," announced the hunchback.

"You?"

"Well, not exactly," said the baker ruefully. "Orestes was handsome and strong, yet he too had a crippling burden to bear." Antonio looked at him inquiringly. The statue had no hunchback.

"His father was murdered when he was a child. He himself was saved only by a miracle and he was taken far away."

"Who was he?" asked Antonio. He was fascinated.

"His mother was Clytemnestra," the hunchback said disapprovingly. "She wanted to marry Aegisthus and make him king."

"And did she?" demanded Antonio.

"Yes. But Orestes returned and killed them both."

"Gosh!"

"People don't always have burdens as obvious as mine, my boy," declared the hunchback, putting the final touches to the little warrior. "Now we leave this to dry and when it is ready we put it in the oven and cook it. Just like the bread." He chuckled. "And when it's done it's just the same color as the crust on a loaf."

Antonio took in every word.

"Now if you want to color it, what you do is rather more complicated. I'll tell you about that another time."

"How do you make cups, and vases?" Antonio asked.

Orestes took another lump of clay, kneaded it a little, then put it on a wide stone wheel and sat down beside it on a small stool. By moving a pedal with his foot he made the stone wheel spin around, and at the same time he shaped the clay into a bowl with his hands. Little by little it grew, like magic. At last it was finished.

"How clever!" Antonio said admiringly.

"Would you like to try?" asked the hunchback. He had clearly made his hump into something good, thought Antonio, not into a sad, ugly thing inside like the invisible hump of the other Orestes, the one Antonio had never heard of.

36

"Tell me about the other Orestes."

"He lived hundreds and hundreds of years ago, but you can still see him today."

Antonio looked at the baker in astonishment.

"Haven't you ever been to the theatre at Syracuse?"

"No, never," Antonio said.

"Ah well, you're young yet," the hunchback said smiling. "Now, how about a try?"

It was Antonio's turn now. He took a piece of the damp clay. It felt heavy and stuck to his fingers. Somehow it didn't seem nearly as easy as when he had been watching Orestes. He tried to pull it into the shape of a bowl, but it turned out all wrong—a pathetic, battered object. He put it on the wheel and started to pedal, but the wheel spun around much too fast; he felt almost giddy and the horrid lump slipped from his fingers.

"Gently now!" cried Orestes, and Antonio managed to get a hold on his masterpiece. "Wet your hand. No, not like that . . . look, it's lopsided. Steady . . . there! Now a bit faster. Good. Well done!"

So Antonio made his first bowl. All right . . . it was a little lopsided and there was an odd bulge at the bottom, but taken as a whole it wasn't too bad. Antonio was very proud of it.

And it's true: to make anything yourself, even an odd-shaped bowl, from the raw materials, is tremendously exciting. Even making bread must feel a bit like that. A man could well make that his life's work and feel proud of it.

Now it was very late. Rinaldo, fortified by a crust of bread which Orestes gave him, managed a steady trot —indeed he almost galloped—all the way home.

As for the secrets learned from Orestes, the kind and generous hunchback, Antonio knew they were safe with him and Rinaldo.

CHAPTER FOUR

Tom Disappears

THE FOUR FRIENDS were down on the beach.

It wasn't the usual sort of beach, for it was covered with a layer of dry seaweed deep enough to make a kind of enormous cushion. You could sink into it and bounce on it as if it were a sofa. A huge outdoor sofa, with the sea for a carpet, right at the end of a triangular island called Sicily—what more could four children and a dog want?

The town square of Marzamemi looked like part of a toy village. There were the little cardboard houses, the two flights of steps that went up to the tiny church on the one side and to the entrance of a miniature palace on the other and, behind it all, the uneven, tumbling hills.

Once upon a time the palace must have been a real

39

one, but now it was in ruins and people drove carts right through it.

At first glance the square seemed completely shut in. But right at the far corner, between two houses—so close together that the average person would have banged his head on their balconies—was a narrow passage which suddenly fell into the sea. That sounds ridiculous. Actually before one got to the sea there was

a neat little row of small boats, then a line of rocks. And then, beyond that, the beach.

Antonio, Rosalia, Giangi and Tom slipped out from this gap between the houses.

Tufty appeared alone from the opposite direction, walking very slowly from behind the farthest rocks way at the end of the beach. He was whistling; his hands were in his pockets and he looked preoccupied.

He was concentrating on walking exactly on the line where the sea met the sand, like a tightrope walker on a wire. All at once he saw something. At the sea's edge, just where he was walking, the waterline seemed to be alive with something pale and pink that was shifting and swaying with the sea. Tufty thought he must be dreaming. He looked more closely. It was a froth of tiny fragments of coral that the sea had torn from the great coral forests far below the waves.

Tufty bent down and gathered up a handful of the tiny grains, all mixed with sand. They were very fragile and seemed almost alive. He was amazed by how beautiful they were. For some time now, Tufty had been making remarkable discoveries of one sort or another, and now it suddenly struck him as miraculous that he should have eyes to see and hands to gather these precious splinters from the great coral trees.

He gave a piercing whistle, and at once Antonio, Rosalia, Giangi and Tom came running, following him barefooted along the line of coral. They collected each grain they could find. Tom was not much help—he trod all over the place and ground the grains into the sand, shaking his head and sneezing to draw attention to himself.

As they were squatting there with heads together, Antonio remarked quietly, almost casually, "I've got my accordion." Giangi was so startled he lost his balance, and Tom began to bark wildly. Antonio looked at Giangi without lifting his head. His eyes were so bright and happy that Giangi wanted to hug him, but he didn't dare because, after all, Antonio was almost grown-up.

"You can tell Turi that now I have my accordion."

Yes! Oh, yes! Giangi nodded. He too had learned that characteristic Sicilian gesture, chin up, lips tight, a faint smile. His parents would never have nodded like that, but Giangi had almost been reborn down here in Sicily and naturally he had learned to behave like his friends.

They pulled off their ragged shirts and shorts and flung themselves into the water. The evening sea was warm but fresh. Tom, however, didn't exactly strip. His woolly coat had been stuck to him at birth and as far as he was concerned it would stay that way. This seemed to him an excellent excuse not to go into the sea; he stayed hesitating on the shore, barking and tearing back and forth. Giangi came out, dripping wet and stark naked, and threw himself on Tom, dragging and shoving him into the water in a way that only a real friend could have dared.

Tom swam very carefully, in the way we often do things we dislike intensely but cannot avoid. Then he turned back, paying no attention to Giangi's orders or the shouts of the others. He had the smug look of one who knows he has done his duty. Back on the beach he was so waterlogged that he could hardly move. He shook himself energetically, showering drops for yards around and then, feeling much lighter, he rolled in the dry seaweed, with the happy result that he looked like a sort of pagan idol, bristling with straw and feathers and bits of string.

All at once another band of children invaded the beach, spilling out of the same alleyway. They yelled and rolled about in the seaweed, worse than Tom, and then started playing catch with Antonio's and Giangi's and Tufty's sandals and threatened to carry off Rosalia's dress. As soon as she realized this she began to swim madly for the shore, followed by the others.

Meanwhile, forgotten by everybody, Tom wandered off to rub himself against the rocks in an attempt to rid himself of the seaweed which he had just so happily collected all over his black coat. He enjoyed this even more.

The children reached the beach and hurled themselves on the culprits. There was a real free-for-all.
But in a few minutes Antonio, Tufty and Giangi (as-
sisted by Rosalia who, although a girl, didn't do at all
badly with her teeth and nails) won the day. The in-
vaders took to their heels and disappeared in a flash,
flinging insults over their shoulders.

But Tom, too, had vanished from the battlefield.

Giangi searched and searched for him, calling, whistling and trying all the pet names he could think of.
But it was no good.

Then he felt afraid. And suddenly so did the others.

They all joined in the search, scouring every corner,
even moving the boats and looking behind the rocks,
and finally trying the village square itself.

Tom was not to be found.

Giangi began to cry, quietly, but with such deep
sobs that it seemed as if his heart would break. "Tom,"
he sobbed very softly, tracing with his fingers any little
mark in the sand that might be a clue. But there was
nothing. Poor Giangi felt all empty inside.

"We *must* find him," Antonio said to Tufty and
Rosalia. His clear eyes were clouded with worry. They
looked at Giangi but did not dare go near him; it's
hard to know what to do when something big goes
wrong.

"Come along," said Rosalia, pulling Giangi's arm.
"Come to Turi."

Giangi let himself be led away. The magic name of Turi suddenly seemed the one thing that could put everything right. He could already almost see Tom again, with his curly black coat, his cold nose and his wagging tail.

They crossed the square and climbed up through the fields toward the dusty hedge of Turi's garden.

Turi was sitting in his doorway braiding straw and whistling. The tune he whistled would perhaps have become famous, if he had only known how to write it down on paper. Instead, with the last twist of straw, it would float away on the wind.

As soon as he saw them in the distance, Turi realized that something must have happened. Something not good.

"Turi!" said Antonio, planting himself in front of the doorway with his hands in his pockets, and motioning toward Giangi with his chin. Giangi stayed hiding behind the others. He did not want Turi to see him crying.

"Giangi," called Turi. He drew him out from the group and placed him between his knees. Giangi hung his head.

"Tom has disappeared." "We can't find him anywhere." "Tom." "The dog." "He's lost." "He's gone." "He must be hiding." "Tom."

They all burst out together. What had happened was so awful they couldn't bear it any longer.

"Tom? What's happened?" demanded Turi. They told him. Or rather Antonio did, while the others stood and listened, making sure that he didn't leave anything out.

"Then he wasn't there anymore."

"We could always get another dog," Turi said when he had heard the story. But Giangi trembled against his knees and Turi's own heart sank. No. Of course not. Tom was Tom and no other dog could possibly take his place.

"Right, then, we'll find Tom. Don't you worry. Giangi, don't worry. Who else was on the beach?" Turi asked.

"There was Raffaele, Ciccio, Nino . . ." said Antonio.

"And Rags," added Tufty.

"Who's Rags?" Turi asked.

"Rags. That's what we call him."

"His real name is Augusto di Calascibetta," said Antonio.

Augusto di Calascibetta was called Rags by everyone because all his clothes seemed to be old and tattered, and looked as if they had been worn by hundreds of people before him. His family were the poorest of the poor. They had only recently moved to the coast from inland, in a desperate attempt to save themselves from starvation.

Rags was a terribly thin boy with sunken cheeks and

deep-set eyes. He was bad-tempered and unbelievably dirty. Rags. Poor Augusto di Calascibetta.

"That horrible boy," said Tufty. "I bet he took Tom."

"It's you who's horrible," Turi said. "If you call him Rags no wonder he wanted to get back at you."

"But everyone calls him that. The way they all call me Tufty."

"That's different. If he's called Rags because he hasn't anything decent to wear he must hate it."

Tufty didn't answer and Turi thought to himself, I just hope nothing awful has happened to poor Tom.

"We'll find him," he said firmly. "Don't worry."

Giangi looked up. Turi would find Tom. He could trust Turi. Turi always made him feel better. "Antonio has his accordion," he whispered, wanting to tell Turi something nice.

Turi's face lighted up. He looked at Antonio. Antonio turned bright red, as if he had a guilty secret. "I haven't exactly got it yet. Tomorrow," he added mysteriously. And they could get nothing more out of him.

That night Giangi had a nightmare. He dreamed that Tom was chained up and howling pitifully; he couldn't lie down or sit or even stretch out, and he was looking at Giangi with imploring eyes. Turi arrived with an enormous pair of pliers and cut the chain. Then Giangi was hugging the black woolly coat and

47

feeling the cold nose on his cheek and he was loving Turi and Tom so hard . . .

But when he woke up there was no Tom. Turi had already left for work and Giangi suddenly felt so alone in the world that he started to cry bitter tears all over the bread and oil and garlic that Turi had left for him on the table.

CHAPTER FIVE

Orestes and the Accordion

It is a complete mystery how Antonio managed to disappear and make his trips to Orestes' bakery without his father's discovering what was going on.

He often had to go on foot, and week after week he gave up any free time he had when he was not out fishing with his father. He would get up early, before dawn, and be home again by the time the boats returned. Or he would slip away during the few precious hours he had to himself during the day. But all this was not really a sacrifice, for nothing seemed too much of an effort if it brought him nearer his goal.

The hunchback had taken him on as an assistant because he knew that Antonio would have had a hard time on his own. He had no oven, no wheel on which to turn his pots; he would have had to find the right

49

sort of clay and know how to knead it. How on earth would poor Antonio have managed?

Besides, Orestes was glad to have a strong boy like Antonio to help him. Antonio was paid a small wage and, what's more, he got a great deal of satisfaction from the arrangement, which is really just as important.

Little by little, Antonio managed to accumulate the amount he needed to buy the accordion. It took months and months of course.

Then, one fine day—the one after Tom disappeared on the beach—Antonio had an appointment with Orestes in Syracuse.

They were going together to buy the accordion.

Orestes had agreed to meet him at half past two by the traffic lights at the edge of Syracuse, on the road from Noto.

Antonio spotted the hunchback from a long way off. He was standing on the street corner.

"Today we are going to see Orestes," the hunchback said as soon as they met.

"What?" exclaimed Antonio in surprise.

"The Orestes of old, the one with the sword."

"Oh!" Antonio was thrilled.

The children had heard a great deal about the Greek theatre at Syracuse, for it was famous, but they had never been there because they never had enough money to buy tickets. Antonio imagined it would be rather like a public storyteller, only on a grander scale, with real people instead of the paper pictures.

And that's how it was.

There was a big audience, crowded onto the semicircular rows of stone steps. Orestes and Antonio arrived early in order to get good seats in the unreserved part, and already they were nearly all taken. Many people were having a picnic lunch, and those who were sitting in the seats in the full glare of the sun were wearing enormous colored straw hats, which they bought off the loaded barrows outside the theatre.

Several boys with trays of orangeade and other cold drinks slung around their necks were clambering up and down the rows. Others, with similar trays or baskets, were selling the book of the *Tragedy of Orestes*.

Orestes bought a copy and began to skim through it while Antonio sat spellbound, gazing at the scene of the magnificent colonnaded palace. Between the audience and stage there was an empty semicircular space, and a sort of altar, richly carved.

"What's that?" asked Antonio.

"Clytemnestra's palace."

"Orestes' mother?"

"In the city of Argos. And that in the middle is the tomb of Agamemnon."

"Orestes' father?"

"Yes, the tomb of his murdered father. But you are going to see how Orestes avenged him."

"Were you ever here when he was killed?"

"Indeed I was. I come to the theatre a lot. King Agamemnon gave such a dreadful cry that it made me shudder from head to toe, and some of the women were in tears. When the poet who wrote about all this was alive you could watch the whole story of Orestes and his family in this very theatre. The performance began much earlier than this and it used to last until nightfall. It must have been wonderful. Nowadays they don't always give a complete version; they leave out lines, sometimes two or three at a time."

"But why?" asked Antonio.

"It takes too much time—and time costs money."

The sun had already passed its height, but was still high in the sky, when the trumpets rang out and a young man dressed as an ancient warrior, but without a shield or sword or helmet, entered with a companion. He went over to Agamemnon's tomb and began to speak.

Antonio's heart leapt. This was Orestes! A real live Orestes talking. Now he saw why the hunchback said Orestes was still alive, after all these centuries.

Twelve women came in, led by a beautiful girl. They were all in black with their hair flowing loose over their shoulders.

"Who are they?" Antonio whispered. The audience, who had been so noisy, excited and talkative, had become quite still; they hardly breathed.

"That is Electra, Orestes' sister, and her friends; they are accompanying her to her father's tomb," whispered Orestes. "They all speak together because they are the chorus. It's as if Aeschylus, the poet, were speaking through their lips."

A murmur rose from the audience. Electra and Orestes had recognized each other and embraced, weeping with emotion.

"Whoever does wrong must pay for it," says an ancient proverb.

"Remember that," the hunchback said to Antonio. In fact everything in this magnificent old tale rang true; it was all as important today as it had ever been.

As he listened, Antonio thought about the sea, and how his father struggled with fish, big and small, to feed his family; and about the bad weather which made fishing dangerous; and about the winter when there had been nothing to eat and the Wolf—a terrible man who was known as the Wolf—had killed a man in the street to rob him and how he had been found hanged from a tree. In fact he thought about all the terrifying things in life and realized that only poets can give them any sense and meaning.

"When did they live, these ancient poets?"

The hunchback tilted his head back, with his chin

sticking out, thinking. "Four, maybe five, hundred years before Christ."

It was terrible to see Orestes, having killed Aegisthus, looking for his mother to kill her too.

The woman sitting next to Antonio—a fishwife from Syracuse to whom he had often sold his fish—shed hot tears, digging her elbow hard into his ribs, though he scarcely noticed.

On the other side, the hunchback seemed transformed.

"Do things like this still happen?" Antonio asked.

"Yes, just like this." Orestes bowed his head in sadness. "He who kills will be killed. Violence only brings more violence." He sighed. "What we have seen was only a few deaths. But war, which means many, many deaths, follows. Violence, brutality, wickedness. There is no need to kill."

Dusk was falling as they returned to Syracuse. The shops were still open and it did not take long to buy the accordion.

Antonio touched it, stared at it; above all he touched it. It just did not seem possible that it could be real.

Orestes led him to the mechanic's where he had left the old truck he used for taking pottery to the market. He bundled Antonio and his accordion into it, and drove back to Marzamemi.

Antonio was so tired that he could not really take in what was happening, or what the little hunchback was doing. Orestes went with him into the house, said a word to his father and departed. Antonio did not even bother to eat, but went straight to bed, taking his accordion with him. He put it at the head of his bed and went to sleep at once, with his hand resting on it.

Orestes had told Antonio's father that the accordion had been honestly obtained, and that if they approved he would take the boy into regular employment with him. They were to think about it and let him know. Antonio's family had been speechless. Then his father had stammered something, perhaps: "He's a good boy, Antonio."

Orestes returned home in his broken-down old truck. Next to him, on the seat, lay a book—*The Choephore*—a tragedy by Aeschylus, poet of ancient Greece.

CHAPTER SIX

Augusto, Otherwise Known as Rags

Sᴜɴᴅᴀʏ. The church bells were ringing, brisk and insistent. At the bottom of the rope was Giuseppangelo
Baroni, known as Tufty, dressed in a cassock and looking as if he were playing some kind of game. The
women were arriving, black shawls over their heads.
Down the paths and between the prickly pears came
the donkeys, their riders dressed in black. The people
dismounted and went into the church, leaving the
donkeys tied up outside. The donkeys looked around
for thistles to munch; there were a few hens to keep
them company but although the square was unpaved
none of them found much to get excited about. Now
and then a hen fluttered onto a little mound, looked
around distractedly, peered eagerly at the ground,
flapped her wings violently as if about to achieve great

things, and then hopped down more dejected than ever. Poor scrawny chickens.

Not far away, behind the houses in the square, the sea was pounding. One day it is calm enough to swim in; the next day it will be raging and a great storm will blow up. Probably it will rain, too. This often happens at the end of May.

On this particular Sunday the sky was threatening.

Everyone, even the men, went into church right at the beginning of the service. After all, it was better in church than outside, just then.

Nobody likes a storm, and it is just as well to pray that it will be only a mild one.

What a pity it is that men are so often moved more by fear than anything else.

The church was crowded when Father Peter started his sermon.

"The seventh commandment is . . . Thou shalt not steal."

Tufty, sitting on a stool near the altar, squirmed about and made such faces at Giangi that anyone could tell there was some secret between them.

"Our tomatoes ripen in the warm sun; they grow red and round and full of goodness. In the same way our souls mature in the sunshine of God's love, when we do good deeds and feel at peace with ourselves. But bad weather can suddenly descend . . ."

The congregation shifted uneasily in their seats. Those at the back, nearest the doors, turned around and looked anxiously up at the sky.

". . . and hail can destroy those same tomatoes, break their tender fragrant skin, turn them rotten and unhealthy. So also our bad deeds, our willful behavior, can turn our souls, our consciences, bad and rotten. Bad and dirty. Remember that."

Father Peter turned around; the sermon was over.

Giangi searched through the congregation until at last he saw, tucked away in a corner, huddled in his ragged old clothes, Augusto di Calascibetta. It seemed that the other boy was staring straight at him. His sunken eyes looked full of spite.

Could Rags really have stolen his dog? At the thought of Tom, tears welled into Giangi's eyes. Through his tears, through those horrid musty old clothes, Giangi seemed to see right into Rags' heart. It looked just like a tomato that was all withered up and shriveled and pockmarked from hailstones.

The Mass was over. Everyone straggled away across the square. The groups were silent, unfriendly, scowling. Those who lived a little way off, in the country or by the sea along the Noto Marina road, mounted their donkeys and disappeared without a word. It was not quite raining.

In the little sacristy Tufty was helping Father Peter take off his vestments. He was so excited that his movements were all jerky. He dashed here and there and put things back to front and lost one of his shoes in the confusion.

"Why all the hurry today?" asked the priest.

"We have to look for Tom, Turi's Giangi's dog," said Tufty, looking up at Father Peter. Then he winked at him, grinned and made his escape.

Outside the others were waiting.

"Where did he go?"

"That way," said Rosalia, who had been instructed to keep her eyes on Rags.

"The Noto road?"

"Yes."

They set off. They took shortcuts that they knew well and at a certain spot they came back onto the road. There was no one to be seen.

"Rosalia, are you sure?"

Rosalia lifted her chin in a gesture much more firm than a simple yes.

"He's probably gone home," said Giangi.

They set off again with Antonio in the lead. Behind him came Tufty, then Giangi and Rosalia.

Suddenly Antonio turned and said, "There are too many of us." Rosalia and Giangi stayed behind, hidden by an olive tree, while Antonio went off in one direction and Tufty in another.

Nearby there was a kind of ravine, with steep sheer sides cut out of the hard rock—the same grayish-gold rock that the theatre was made of. Two or three of the very poorest families from inland—where things were even worse—had set up living quarters there for want of anything better. Among them was Augusto, known as Rags.

Antonio and Tufty moved forward with great care so as not to be seen. The place was strangely silent and lifeless. If the boys had not known for sure that the mossy wall of the ravine was in fact the front of a "house" they would never have believed anyone could live in such a hole.

There was only one clue—a rusty pipe sticking out of a hole beside an opening which presumably was a door. From the pipe came a feeble wisp of smoke. Heaven only knew what such a pathetic fire could be cooking.

Suddenly the air was torn by the sound of a voice. It was a voice that cracked and broke hoarsely, a voice that simply couldn't belong to either man or woman.

It scared Antonio.

A pathetic, terrified little figure shot out of the caves, with the awful voice in pursuit. It was Rags. He stood huddled in his shapeless musty clothes, his back turned on the stream of abuse. He was sobbing, but his eyes were dry. There were no tears.

The owner of the voice appeared. It was a woman, thin and dirty, as broken as the sounds she made. She looked around her and, when her eye fell on her son, she went at him again, getting more and more hoarse and breathless. When Rags, as if to aggravate her, stood motionless, she came at him with a heavy ladle, which made him cover his head with his arms to protect himself. At last he did move away, but he did not run; he limped, sobbing dry, frantic sobs. "Beg. Beg. I will not do it."

Was it really Rags who spoke? The boy passed within a few feet of Antonio without seeing him.

Antonio would not have recognized him. Was this Augusto di Calascibetta, known as Rags, usually so cocky, so impudent, so ready to yell insults and make faces? This?

On a sudden impulse Antonio ran after him and when he caught up asked point-blank; "What have you done with our dog?"

Rags turned around. No, in fact he whipped around like a little snake showing its forked tongue. In that instant he was transformed. This was the usual Rags.

"I sold him," he answered defiantly.

By now Tufty had arrived. Momentarily losing control, Antonio raised his fist. "You monster!" Rags, with an instinctive and clearly habitual reaction, raised his arm to protect his face. It was skinny and covered with bruises.

Tufty, like Antonio just before, seemed suddenly to see a different and somehow pathetic Rags. He looked at the bruises and stopped Antonio's fist. "Wait."

"Why did you do it?" demanded Antonio, now calm again.

Rags lifted his chin in defiance and would not speak.

"Let's take him to Turi," suggested Tufty.

Rags took to his heels, darting between the boys like an arrow. But they were stronger than he was; they chased after him and grabbed him. In spite of his kicking and scratching and biting they managed to collar him and lead him off.

When Giangi saw them coming, he felt suddenly quite sure that Rags was the culprit. He looked just like a criminal between two policemen. It all seemed rather serious; he felt more surprised than angry.

Antonio and Tufty jerked their heads and said, "To Turi." Giangi and Rosalia silently agreed, holding hands as if to comfort each other. They felt as if they were going to a funeral.

Turi was busy preparing a meal in his smoky kitchen. When he saw them coming, his heart skipped a beat; to him too the group looked just like a prisoner with his guards.

"Oh there you are," he said as if nothing had happened.

"It's him who sold him."

"Sold what?"

"Our dog."

The charge was quite definite. Turi straightened up and left the pots on the stove.

"I'll handle this," he said to Antonio quietly. "Good-bye, kids. See you this afternoon."

They all felt somehow disappointed. They had been half afraid of what might happen and now nothing had.

But their faith in Turi was stronger than their surprise. They had complete trust in him.

"Today's Sunday. There's spaghetti for lunch. Would you like some?"

Turi ladled it out. There was tomato sauce with it, and herbs. It was very good.

Rags raised his hungry eyes to the third plate on the table. It was for him.

"Sit down and eat." Turi almost forced him to sit down.

Giangi sat down opposite. He stared across the table so hard that his eyes bulged.

What on earth was Turi doing? Augusto had stolen Tom, his own Tom, his best friend. Giangi believed in Turi. Only he didn't understand what Turi was up to. He didn't understand at all.

Rags was not eating. Just the smell of that delicious spaghetti made his head swim. He had never seen anything like it. For two days he had hardly eaten. But he too didn't understand. What made Turi behave like this?

"Are you hungry?" Turi asked.

Augusto nodded.

"Well then, eat," said Turi.

At the first mouthful Rags thought he might faint. It was too good. Then he began really to taste the flavor and to feel better. He lifted his eyes from his plate and looked at Giangi. Giangi looked back at him. Turi held out a large chunk of bread and Rags clutched it, without saying a word. Spaghetti and bread. And tomato sauce. It was fantastic. He must make the most of it, because tomorrow he would hardly believe it had happened. It certainly wouldn't happen again in a hurry.

As soon as they had finished, Turi told Giangi to go and find Antonio and to stay with him. Giangi did as he was told.

Rags slid off his chair and started to disappear, too. Turi stopped him.

"Come here." As he took the boy by the arm he noticed the bruises. "Do they beat you?" he asked.

Augusto di Calascibetta jerked his head, his lips tight shut. He meant yes.

"Who, your mother?"

Another nod.

"And your father?"

65

"He's always drunk."

These were the first words he had spoken. Rags looked about him in desperation, ashamed of this admission and astonished at himself.

"Don't they give you enough to eat?"

A jerk meaning no.

"Why did you sell the dog?"

Silence.

"It wasn't yours."

Silence.

"Whom did you sell him to?"

"They tried to make me go out and beg." There. It was out. He had let it out in one breath, in one second, his disgrace. The thing that haunted him more than anything else in the world, more than the beatings, more than the horrible rags he had to wear, more than his hunger.

Turi sighed. He rose and, rummaging in a cupboard, pulled out a pair of shorts and a worn, faded, striped shirt. "Put these on." Rags stood quite still; his eyes lighted up, uncertain, unbelieving.

"They're for you. I'm giving them to you."

"Mine?"

"Yours."

"Forever?"

This time it was Turi who silently nodded.

Rags dropped his musty tatters and turned shyly

away to put on the shorts and then the shirt. He ran his hand lovingly over his new outfit. If he had not felt a little self-conscious he would have puffed out his chest in pride. Instead he stood very still. But now he could look Turi in the face.

"They are sending you out to beg?"

Augusto lifted his chin in agreement.

"Who?"

"Them."

"Your father and mother?"

A silent yes.

"Where?"

"Syracuse. My brothers are there too."

"Your brothers too?"

"Yes."

"And you live on what they get?"

"It isn't very much."

That certainly rang true. Turi sighed again. Then very patiently he went back to the interrogation. "Why did you take Tom?"

Rags looked obstinately up at the ceiling.

"Whom did you sell him to?"

Silence.

"Surely they paid you something?"

"They are *going* to pay me—a lot of money."

This too slipped out against his will. It was the child in him speaking, not the sly, nasty thing he had grown to be. In some respects Augusto would never be a child again.

"Are you sure they'll pay you?"

A sudden flash of suspicion showed in Rags' face. This was what Turi had been waiting for. But still Rags was silent.

Turi shrugged his shoulders. "All right then. Off you go," he said. Rags bundled his musty old clothes under his arm and started away slowly, almost regretfully. When he reached the door he stopped, turned slowly around and looked at Turi. Turi looked back at him intently, holding his breath. Rags hung his head and whispered under his breath, "Rocco and Nino from Noto."

Turi was filled with relief; he drew a deep breath. He hardly knew whether he was more glad to have news of Tom or finally to have wrung the confession from Rags just when he was beginning to give up hope.

"Do they already have the dog?" he asked, trying to seem matter-of-fact. He began to tidy the room, fetching hot water from the stove and pouring it over the plates into a metal basin.

"Yes." Rags looked at Turi. His eyes were full of the suspicion that had begun to dawn a few seconds ago.

"Ah," said Turi.

"Why?" demanded Rags, his bundle under his arm. He turned and planted himself beside the sink.

"Are you sure they'll pay you?"

"They are going to meet me this evening at"—now he really had said too much—"a place I know."

"Wouldn't you like me to come with you?" Turi ventured to ask. There was really no telling how to handle this wild little creature.

"What for?" asked Rags, running a finger along the edge of the basin, his other hand in his pocket—the first pocket he had ever had.

"Well, I could give you a hand if those two didn't want to pay up."

Even Rags was beginning to feel that Turi was someone to be trusted. He hesitated a moment more. "Do you want the money for yourself?" he asked.

Turi laughed out loud as he dried the three chipped plates and the tin forks. "All right, I won't come. You sort things out for yourself with those two rats."

Rags suddenly looked a little like Giangi when he wanted Turi beside his bed before he would go to sleep. When he finally gave way and asked Turi to help, his voice too was a little like Giangi's.

"Come with me, Turi."

He was far too small to deal with anything so big all by himself. They would go together.

CHAPTER SEVEN

Rendezvous at Night

A LITTLE WAY up the coast from Marzamemi toward Noto Marina, here and there are little deserted coves full of rocks and hollows and fine, fine sand. They can be reached by car, along paths which go right down to the seashore.

The appointment with Rocco and Nino from Noto— who had a station wagon—was at one of these inlets just past Marzamemi, at ten o'clock at night.

A thieves' rendezvous.

Turi and Rags, who was once more bundled up in some of his ragged old clothes to keep out the damp, set off at about nine thirty, when all Marzamemi was already silent and fast asleep.

They made their way without a word. Turi had a flashlight to help them over the tricky places. Soon they would not need it, for the moon would be up. It

70

was cool, and the grass—where there was any—was wet with dew.

At last they reached the spot where the ground sloped down to the little cove. Turi shone the flash, and the sudden light sent a crowd of rabbits scurrying hither and thither under their feet, in and out of the bushes and around the rocks. They were gone in an instant.

Turi and Rags scrambled down and sat themselves on a boulder with a round top like the shell of some giant tortoise.

The moon was rising and the sands shone clear and white. All was quiet. Even the lapping of the sea was soft, gentle as the tongue of a cow licking her newborn calf.

Far away in the distance they heard the sound of a car on the road to Noto. But no trains whistled on the rails nearby. Nothing.

"If they don't come, then what will you do?" asked Turi at last.

"Those rats," muttered the boy. He was very pale, as white as the moonlit sand.

Time passed. The moon rose high in the sky.

Rags had stopped leaping to his feet and listening hopefully each time it seemed as if a car might be coming a little closer. He might almost have been asleep, except that his eyes were wide open.

71

"What you did was wrong, you know," Turi found himself saying, rather to his surprise.

Rags didn't seem surprised at all. He replied at once, "It was better than begging."

"That has nothing to do with it," said the man. "It was still the wrong thing to do."

"They told me, 'If you get us Turi's dog we'll sell it for a lot of money and pay you for it.'"

"So, it had to be *my* dog?"

"They say they are rich people's dogs, that kind. The Baroness Lalumia, at Noto, has been looking for a dog like that."

"Have they sold him to her?"

Rags shrugged his shoulders. He had no idea.

"If they don't show up, we'll go to Noto together tomorrow."

"Rats!" Rags repeated to himself through clenched teeth.

"How would you like to play the mouth organ?"

Rags tilted his head to the sky and raised his eyebrows in a hopeless gesture meant to express something like this: "How on earth could I, Augusto di Calascibetta, known as Rags—and Rags I shall be all my life, even if I do now have a decent shirt and shorts—how on earth could *I* ever hope to do that?"

"I could teach you," Turi said. There was a pause. "If you would like."

Rags looked at him again in the darkness—for the moon was beginning to go down.

He had the same look on his face as when Turi had given him his new clothes.

"Let's go home," said Rags jumping up. "They're rats, that's all." Turi stood up.

Behind them it seemed almost as if the giant boulder had got up too and was lumbering into the sea like a great tortoise. Anything was possible just then.

Rags thrust his hand through his bundle of rags and put it in Turi's to keep him company as they retraced their steps along the sand and through the bushes on the way home.

Their long wait together had done something, after all.

CHAPTER EIGHT

Tom Is Found

Next day, Turi, Giangi and Rags caught the rattly old bus which runs from Pachino to Noto. They hoisted themselves onto it and settled down on the cracked, blistered seats.

When Turi got home the night before he had found Giangi wide awake and waiting for him.

"Was it Rags?" Giangi asked timidly.

"Yes," Turi replied. "But not really him."

"Who else then?"

"It's the fault of a whole lot of things all mixed up together. One day I'll explain it to you. At the moment Rocco and Nino from Noto have got Tom." Rocco and Nino from Noto; how nasty they sounded, those names. Giangi closed his eyes disconsolately. Never, oh never, would he get his Tom back.

Turi stood by Giangi's bed and took his hand—even smaller and more helpless than Rags'. "Go to sleep," he said. "Tomorrow we'll go to Noto and get Tom back."

If Turi said so, there was some hope.

"Go to sleep now. Go to sleep." Giangi was already asleep, dreaming that he was holding one of Tom's soft ears.

When Giangi saw Rags, he hardly recognized him. Who *would* have known him, dressed as he was now?

"Aren't you Rags anymore?" he demanded when he was near enough.

"No," Augusto answered proudly.

Giangi knew that Rags was only a little to blame. He didn't understand how, but Turi had said so, and that was enough.

The bus bounced and jolted up the hill and arrived in the square at Noto. It unloaded its passengers right at the foot of the two great flights of steps leading up to the two churches standing side by side.

Rocco and Nino lived near the square; they had a garage and rented out cars. But it was clear this wasn't their only business. Giangi was right; in fact everyone knew about them. They had a very bad name.

Turi planned to send Rags ahead, as if he were all by himself, to ask about the dog.

When he reached the entrance to the garage, a sort of black den reeking of oil and gasoline, Rags turned and made a little sign to Turi. He certainly seemed quite a different boy now. Giangi was shaking with fright. He willed and willed with all his might that Tom would be inside there somewhere, behind a spare wheel or tied to a jack. Tom, his black coat gray with engine oil, his eyes shining and his little tail wagging.

Suddenly Rags shot out of the workshop, whirled around and shook his fist. Livid with rage, he shouted, "You rats!" Rocco followed, also brandishing his fist, his brawny arms filthy with grease. "Rat yourself. Get out and don't let me catch you here again!"

Rags moved off a little; suddenly he spun around and spat in the dust. Rocco made as if to chase him. The boy took to his heels and rejoined Turi and Giangi at the corner of the street. "The rats!" he panted. He was purple in the face.

"Tom?" asked Giangi.

Rags shook his head. "He wasn't there. They've already sold him."

"To Baroness Lalumia?" asked Turi.

Rags shrugged his shoulders miserably, implying that he didn't know anything more. He winced. "He hit me," he said, rubbing his shoulder.

"Let's go and see the Baroness Lalumia," Turi said.

Skirting the walls of the prison, they went down the street where, on certain days, the market was held, and turned to the left.

At that very moment, a long, black car came out through the gateway of the Lalumia palace. The driver was wearing black, there was black mourning crepe across the back window, and the people inside were all in black.

Turi went up to the gateway. Another piece of black crepe was hanging there; it would stay there until it became gray with dust, if it hadn't fallen to pieces by then.

A little old man—all in black too, except for his sparse, silver hair—was sitting on a chair outside the gateway, enjoying the sun.

"Excuse me," said Turi.

"What?"

"Excuse me," repeated Turi, clearing his throat. "Is the Baroness Lalumia at home?"

"Eh?" The old man was deaf and couldn't understand him.

"I asked, is the Baroness at home?" bellowed Turi. Giangi laughed and Rags made a face.

"The old Baroness, yes, but she's not seeing anyone," replied the old man calmly.

"It's very urgent," persisted Turi.

"Who? Who wants to see her?" asked the old man.

"Us," Turi replied promptly.

The man pointed vaguely toward the palace, and the three of them made their way to a magnificent marble staircase that led up from the cool, dark entranceway.

They went up. At the top was a wide terrace with three doors. They knocked and knocked, but no one came. They tried again. At last there was a shuffle of footsteps and a very old woman in soft felt slippers opened the door a crack and peeped out. "Who is it?"

"Good morning," Turi said, taking off his hat. "I should like to see the Baroness. It's rather urgent."

"The Baroness is not at home. She has gone with the Baron in the car to Syracuse."

"Could I perhaps have a word with the old Baroness?"

"She no longer sees anyone since the death of her husband, the old Baron Lalumia."

"Please tell her I'm here," insisted Turi. "It's about the dog."

"About the dog?" said the old woman eying him suspiciously. "What dog? They have already brought us one, yesterday morning."

Turi squeezed Giangi's hand. "That's just what I've come about. The dog was stolen from me."

The woman seemed impressed and finally opened the door. "Come in. I will tell the Baroness." And she disappeared.

Turi, Giangi and Rags looked around nervously. There were books on every wall, in glass-fronted cases, and heavy hangings at the windows.

The maid reappeared as silently as she had vanished. "Please come this way." They followed her.

The old Baroness Lalumia was sitting in a big chair in a drawing room cluttered with furniture. She was a tiny, wrinkled old lady, with white hair and dressed entirely in black except for a collar of white lace high around her throat.

Turi and the children stood nervously in the middle of the room.

The baroness greeted them pleasantly and Turi replied. Then she raised her eyeglass and looked them over. She invited them to sit down, but the children were shy. Turi sat down and they remained standing near his chair.

"You are not from Noto, are you?" the Baroness asked Turi.

"No, your ladyship, we are really from Marzamemi."

"Agata tells me you have come about the dog."

"Yes, your ladyship."

"What's the trouble?" asked the old lady.

"The dog was stolen from us," said Turi. "And I know it was sold to you or someone in your family by Rocco and Nino Burruso."

The Baroness rang a little bell which she had beside her. "Agata, bring the dog here," she said to the maid.

There was a moment's suspense and then the door opened. Tom's paws slithered uncertainly on the polished floor. He looked miserable, his ears drooping and his nose hot and dry. But as soon as he realized Giangi was there he leaped on him with such a frantic display of affection that he almost knocked him over.

Giangi burst into tears of joy, crying his dog's name, hugging him and burying his face in the warm fur— that is, when he was able to dodge the bath of wet kisses Tom was giving his nose, his ears, his eyes, and anywhere else he could reach.

There was no question.

The Baroness watched in silence. Then she said, "The dog belongs to the child, that is easy to see. I should never have trusted those Burruso fellows."

"I'm very sorry about this unhappy business, your ladyship," Turi said. "But you see, Tom is Tom, and there can be no other dog for Giangi."

The Baroness Lalumia smiled. "Of course. I understand. I have some grandchildren—in fact it was because of them that I let myself accept the Burrusos' offer. They were so eager to have a dog. Now we have been punished for our impatience, and we shall have to wait until we can find another. As for the Burrusos . . ."

Turi held his breath. Instinctively he put his hand on Rags' shoulder. He had to protect him, for who else would? The Burruso brothers would certainly do anything they could to shift the blame from themselves.

"You may leave the Burrusos to me. I'll get back the

money you gave them, your ladyship. And I'll bring it here to you," Turi said.

"But . . . that should be my concern," suggested the Baroness.

"Don't give it another thought, please, your ladyship," Turi replied. "Those two are—"

"Rats!" cried Rags, beside himself.

The old lady smiled.

"Agata!" she called. "The biscuits." Agata brought in a plateful.

"Are these your children?" asked the Baroness Lalumia, passing the biscuits around.

"Yes, your ladyship. That is . . . not exactly. I am not really their father, but I think of them as mine. They live with me."

A little later the Baroness said good-bye.

They left, with Tom trotting behind them.

"Wait for me in the square, and don't run off," Turi said firmly to Giangi and Rags. He set off along the road, which was dusty white in the sun and quite deserted at that hour.

The Burruso brothers' garage looked more like a wild animal's den than a workshop.

Nino was stretched out under a shabby old car, the kind you can hire by the hour or for the day. Rocco was over at the workbench filing away furiously at something, the sweat running down his neck to the mat of black hair on his chest. "And where is my dog?" demanded Turi, wisely staying on the threshold. Rocco looked up.

"Your dog? I never set eyes on your dog."

"Oh yes you did, when you sold him to the Baroness Lalumia," said Turi a bit louder.

"He comes to our own doorway to insult us, the lout! He's got some nerve!" shouted Rocco, raising the file in a threatening way.

Nino crawled out from under the car. He had a large spanner in his hand. "What do you want?" he asked.

"The man's crazy," Rocco said. But he had an ugly look on his face. "Come in, come in and let's talk it over," said Nino. He sounded almost friendly.

Turi, be careful. Watch out, Turi. Turi heard a warning voice inside him which he knew he should obey. He moved forward a little, as if to enter, but he didn't go in.

Rocco raised the file.

There was a split-second pause, and then Turi, with a speed which surprised even himself, punched Rocco hard in the stomach. Big and heavy as he was, he gasped and staggered back, crashing into a pile of tires which fell on top of him.

Rocco swore horribly and hurled himself at Turi.

Nino stopped him. "Are you mad? Here, in the

middle of town? Do you want to get us into trouble?"

"Get out, you filthy peasant, get out or I'll kill you!" bellowed Rocco, who had dropped the file and was clutching his stomach.

"Ah, so you'll kill me, will you?" cried Turi, his fist aching and his temper flaring. "You're a thief, so you might as well become a murderer; there's not much risk in it. Two against one. With weapons in your hands. . . . I'm going down to call the police, and then we'll see."

Turi backed away and turned down the street. He set off through the dust.

Behind in their lair the brothers were arguing. Perhaps they were quarreling. This is often the way with partners in crime.

Then Turi heard Nino's voice calling, "Stop! Wait a minute!"

He did not even look around.

Rocco came out of the shop and followed him down the road. Turi heard him come up behind, panting heavily, and had to control a strong urge to run for it. Turi, you are not afraid, said the voice. You must not be afraid.

"Stop," said Rocco, "or you'll be sorry."

Turi did not answer. He kept walking.

"Come back, and let's talk it over with Nino," Rocco insisted. Still there was no answer. They had almost reached the police station. Along the wall a strip of shadow showed black against the white, dusty road.

Turi knew that the hatred of the Burruso brothers was now well and truly roused. It was nasty, but he had to go through with it. If he showed any sign of fear, it would be even worse. And it might involve Rags, too.

Just as he was about to turn in at the entrance, Rocco seized his arm. "If you keep quiet, I'll give you back the money."

Turi stopped.

Rocco gave a gasp of relief. "Let's go back to the garage. Nino has the money."

"No," said Turi. "You bring the money here to me. I'm not going back to your den to get myself killed."

Rocco hesitated a moment. Then he turned around. Nino was standing in the doorway, his hands on his hips.

Turi did not move. Rocco made his way slowly back to the shop, slouching along like a whipped dog.

Turi watched him out of the corner of his eye. I've got away with it, he thought. Right now I could be flat on my face in the dust, beaten to pulp. He stood his ground and waited. Outwardly he was the picture of courage. And that was what mattered.

Rocco came back and, looking cautiously around, slipped the money into Turi's hand. Between clenched teeth he muttered, "You'll pay for this. Just remember that."

Turi did not flinch and went on his way along the wall of the police station. His heart was pounding. At the Lalumia palace he quickly handed over the money to Agata, the maid, who looked at him in astonishment. Then he rejoined the children.

Giangi and Rags had crossed the road and were standing gazing up at a huge colored poster. A boy with a dog, who looked exactly like Tom, was eating a magnificent ice cream.

Turi went over to them and his eye fell on the poster next door. It was for a competition.

NATIONAL CONTEST
FOR BANDMASTERS' POSTS
RULES OF ENTRY (etc., etc.)
DOCUMENTS REQUIRED (etc.)

Scholarship for course of Musical Instruction in Specialist Institute in Milan. Repayment of fares to the capital to sit for preliminary examinations etc., etc.)

Turi's heart leapt, but for a different reason this time. What if he should enter? What if he should try, just this once, to challenge fate and fortune and just about all the other would-be bandmasters in Italy?

He wrote down the details on a scrap of paper.

But his first wave of enthusiasm soon drained away at the thought of the almost unthinkable difficulties there would be.

He put the children and the dog onto the bus. As he helped them climb up, something suddenly struck him; from now on he was responsible for two human beings, not one. The responsibility for Giangi, which he had taken on several years before, was now exactly doubled. Now there was Rags, too.

CHAPTER NINE

Seashells

Turi was thinking hard as he conducted his little band. Should he enter this competition? It would be madness. But if he didn't? That would be madness, too. For, as the saying goes: "Nothing venture, nothing win." What chance did he have of winning? Very little, if any. He was almost entirely self-taught. They would ask him about musical theory, and what did he know about that? He could buy a book in Noto, and in the evenings after work . . . but it would take a great deal of determination. However, without that you don't get anywhere.

"Antonio, you went wrong in the bass notes there. Be careful. Now once again from the beginning."

The funniest sight was Giangi, red in the face, his lips tight around the gently vibrating "marranzanu."

In his heart Turi felt that it was his duty to try, for it wasn't as if he had only himself to consider. If he

88

succeeded he would be better able to help those whom chance, or destiny, had entrusted to his care.

Recently the little orchestra had been making great strides. Turi taught each of the four children separately and then brought them together. With very good results, considering what could be expected from a guitar, a tambourine, and a marranzanu. And of course his own clarinet.

The marranzanu stopped abruptly. Tom slowly wagged his tail. Turi turned toward the garden gate. Rags' dark eyes were peeping through the dusty hedge. (They still called him Rags although he now had some decent clothes.)

He would stand there by the hour, watching and listening. They had not yet managed to tame him completely. But Turi noticed that now and then Giangi, Tom and Rags would go off together for a quiet walk by the sea or through the fields. Despite what had happened, they were beginning to understand one another and to make friends.

Turi made no attempt to interfere; he just waited.

Today, at last Rags opened the gate a crack and slipped inside. He stayed right up against the hedge, but on the garden side this time, not outside as he had so often done.

The children were tempted to stop playing and watch him, but Turi kept them going.

Rags crept up to Giangi; now there was only Tom

between them. Tom was sitting up alertly like a good dog, and not missing a note. Rags took his hand shyly from the pocket of his old shorts and put it on the dog's curly head. Tom seemed to like this and wagged his tail from side to side along the ground, slowly so as not to create a disturbance, but still scattering the dust, which lay thick and fine as sand all over the place.

The lesson came to an end.

Antonio ran off. He was now working regularly for Orestes the hunchback. His father had not only given his permission, but was extremely proud that his son had found independent work. He no longer had to rely on the hazardous business of fishing or the back-breaking toil of the fields. Antonio still found time to help at home and his father, to reward him, allowed him to keep part of the wages Orestes paid him, and would also lend him the donkey whenever it was possible. If there were any fish to sell, it was now Antonio's job. Syracuse and Noto were both practically on the road to Floridia.

"Killing two birds with one stone," his father would say cheerfully.

Rosalia hurried away, too. One of her older sisters— the one who was a hairdresser in Syracuse—was getting married. She was marrying the owner of the shop —a piece of great good luck. The family was doing all it could to provide a small trousseau for her; and

Rosalia would sit on a small footstool hemming the edges of a huge sheet. Rosalia was a clever girl and needed little teaching when it came to sewing and embroidery. She was going to miss her sister, who had been like a mother to her.

Tufty was hoping that no one would have noticed his absence from the vineyard where they were gathering the grapes to make Muscat wine—the best wine in the world, so sweet that it was like a liqueur.

Tufty was unaware that his father considered any help from him worse than useless. By now he was resigned to this son of his who was so brilliant at school and a little "cuckoo." Of course, way inside he was really very proud of him, and had secret hopes that one day . . . who knows?

Only Giangi, the dog and Rags were left in Turi's bare little garden.

Turi looked at them.

Giangi was teaching Rags to play the marranzanu and Tom was watching attentively, raising first one floppy ear and then the other. He wondered anxiously whether they would want him to dance on his hind legs as he had learned to do.

Turi had a sudden flash and knew that he simply must enter the competition. He went inside, fetched his identity card, his cap and his wallet containing a few lire. He would go to Noto and get the necessary papers.

On his way out he said to the children, "Be good now. I am going to Noto, but I'll be back soon. Rags, look after Giangi. Tom, be a good dog." Tom jumped all over him and then waited by the gate and watched until Turi had disappeared around the bend of the path.

Rags laid a protective hand on Giangi's shoulder.

"Shall we go and look for shells?" Giangi suggested.

"What for?" asked Rags.

"I've got lots of them. Beautiful ones. Look." Giangi displayed his treasures and Rags was delighted.

"How beautiful," he said, fingering them gently. "I like this one." It looked as if it were made of the finest porcelain, with folds, like a fan. And what a color! Dark pink fading delicately into white.

"Beautiful," Rags whispered again.

"Do you like it?" asked Giangi.

Rags nodded silently.

"I'll give it to you then." Giangi thrust it into his hand. Rags said nothing, but his eyes filled with tears.

He put the shell in his pocket and while they walked toward the sea he stroked it as if it were alive.

"I'm looking for the big one that has all the sea inside it and you can hear it singing," confided Giangi. "But I've never found it yet."

"Shells are too small to have all the sea inside them," said Rags.

"But it's true," Giangi insisted. "Don Pietro had one.

He held it to my ear and the sea really was inside. I want one like it."

"If I find one I'll give it to you," Rags said.

They made their way through the fields until they reached the deserted little beach where Rags and Turi had waited in vain for the Burruso brothers that night.

The sand was smooth and even, and damp between the rocks, which really did look like giant tortoises.

At first glance there didn't seem to be any shells. But Giangi knew that they were hidden here and there in the sand, at the water's edge, or farther off where it was dry. Some of the most beautiful ones were even to be found under the bushes. He knew that the shells were alive, and hid themselves because they didn't always want to be picked up.

"Go seek, Tom," commanded Giangi. Tom gave a little yelp of delight and rushed off to scratch around, covering his nose with damp sand. Rags looked at him curiously. "He understood."

"Of course," said Giangi, crouching down to look, with his head between his knees.

Tom barked softly, and Giangi ran over to him. "This is a shell for you, Tom." It was a magnificent bone, polished with age, the ends blackening slightly —a treasure. "Do you promise to keep on looking afterward?" asked Giangi, holding the bone high in the air. Tom, standing on his hind legs, did a little dance. He looked like a clown in a black fur coat. "Promise, you naughty dog?" Tom gave an expressive whine: he had decided to promise. Giangi laughed and gave him the bone and hugged him.

Rags was all eyes. "He talks!" he murmured.

"Of course he talks," said Giangi, once again intent on the search.

"But how do you understand him?" asked Rags, coming closer and squatting down with his head between his skinny knees. "Is it difficult?" He sounded anxious.

Giangi looked up in astonishment and stared at him. "Is what difficult?"

"Talking to Tom."

"You try."

Tom had been digging an enormous hole in which he had given his magnificent bone a ceremonial burial.

"Try," repeated Giangi.

"What shall I say?" asked Rags with embarrassment, but quietly so that the dog would not hear him.

Giangi nodded encouragingly toward Tom. He had his arm affectionately around the dog's neck.

"Hello," ventured Rags uncertainly. Tom looked at him in amazement. "He doesn't answer *me*."

"He doesn't know you very well yet," Giangi said. "Tom, this is Augusto, whom we call Rags although he's very neat now. He is my friend. Say 'how do you do.' "

94

Tom hesitated, looking doubtfully from one to the other.

"I told you he's my friend. Say hello to him."

Tom offered his right paw, after a slight hesitation over which one to choose. Rags took it and shook it hesitantly.

"Now he knows you. You can say what you like to him," said Giangi. "He won't say 'how do you do' to just anybody, you know."

"He did to *me*," Rags said proudly.

"Yes."

"Oh what a lovely shell," Rags exclaimed suddenly. It was blue all over, really exquisite. He lifted it out of its wet nest in the sand and ran to wash it in the nearest bit of shallow sea. Then he presented it to Giangi with a lordly gesture. "A present," he said.

Even if it wasn't *the* extraordinary shell with all the sea inside it, it was certainly something special. Rags was as proud of his present as if the whole universe had been his to give to whom he wished.

Tom had wriggled free from his master's embrace and was running all over the place like a mad thing. Giangi picked up some flat stones and threw them into the sea, trying to make Tom go out and look for them. "Go get them, Tom." Tom ran to the edge of the sea and stopped, barking. Giangi laughed. "He doesn't want to go into the sea, the bad dog," and he chased him, pretending he was going to throw him in. Tom slipped between his hands and barked, still refusing to go in. Now Rags was laughing again.

And then they found the sea horse.

Giangi had gone to pick up another stone and try to persuade Tom to chase it into the water. Instead he found the sea horse. He stood up, looking at it. Tom wagged his tail, waiting, looking at his master. Rags came over and they looked at it together. It was perfect, from its pointed little face down to its tiny curled tail, and rather pathetic.

Just one small thing from that mysterious life down there, at the bottom of the sea. With its light veins—not scales, not bones, but little ripples which seemed to have been traced by the waves—it was a monster reduced to such a tiny scale that it had become a delightful plaything, a toy.

"What is it?" asked Rags.

Giangi eyed it doubtfully; he didn't know. But they had found something very beautiful. There was no doubt about that.

The search was interrupted. They laid the shells out on one of the tortoise-shaped rocks, together with a starfish which had lost one point and, in the place of honor, the marvelous little sea monster.

Then the two children stood back and admired their treasures.

CHAPTER TEN

Revenge

Turi RETURNED to Pachino on the same bumpy old bus, and walked the rest of the way back to Marza-memi.

The house was deserted and so was the garden. There was no sign of Giangi, or Tom, or Rags.

He put the receipts for his documents away. The necessary papers would be ready in a few days.

He went out into the garden to have a look at his tomatoes, which he had put out on trays covered with a clean cloth to dry in the sun. He lifted a corner; all was well. It would be a couple of days still before the tomatoes, which were salted and sprinkled with cloves of garlic, were ready to put in oil. It was a most important part of the recipe that they should have the right amount of sun.

Behind him Turi heard the sound of panting, and then a scratching noise at the wooden gate. Then came a miserable whine.

Turi went to open the gate. It was Tom. All alone. Tom with the pathetic look of a dog who has seen something horrid. Turi felt a sudden pang of fear.

"Tom, where's Giangi?" he asked. Tom whined and turned to go back the way he had come. He scratched at the gate, asking to be let out again.

"Come here," ordered Turi. His heart was pounding. Tom didn't move, but kept scratching at the gate and whining, on and on, turning beseeching eyes on Turi as if to say, "Try to understand!"

Turi began to sweat with a cold, terrible fear. He ran to open the gate and Tom shot away, down the Noto road, running like a hare. He paused now and then just to make quite sure that Turi was following. Turi's knees felt weak. He stumbled as he ran, and his teeth were clenched in panic. Something was wrong; something horrible had happened.

The sea? But they could both swim. Cramp? Some other disaster? A child can go under so quickly. But Tom was not heading toward the sea. "Blessed Saint Agatha, I promise you an offering . . . not a very big one because I haven't any money . . . but I promise you something for your feast day, if only Tom has just lost them somewhere. No. He knows exactly where he's going. Perhaps something has happened to Rags."

Now they were running along the Noto road. It was almost dark. Turi was about to give up when he saw Tom stop by something.

It was Rags, unconscious at the side of the road. Tom, his tongue hanging out, was scrambling slowly and carefully down into the ditch that ran alongside. He whined. Giangi was lying there, very still. Turi thought he was dead, and for a moment his mind went blank and everything seemed to go black.

But Giangi was breathing. Turi lifted him up and carried him out of the ditch. Then he wiped his face with his handkerchief, terrified that he might find blood, but there was none. The same went for Rags. Finally Giangi opened his eyes, saw Turi and smiled.

"How do you feel? Are you all right? What happened?" Turi was speaking as much to himself as to Giangi.

"The truck," stammered Giangi. "Rags . . ."

He closed his eyes again, dazed. Turi tried to lift Rags, who came to for an instant, groaning, then fainted again. Turi's heart sank. He began to be afraid again. Suddenly a car appeared down the road from the direction of Noto. Turi stood up and waved his arms desperately to get it to stop. A few yards away it pulled up and out got Antonio with Orestes. He had been working late and Orestes was taking him home.

"What's happened?" they asked, terrified. The headlights picked out the two children lying on the ground with Tom standing guard over them.

"I don't know, I don't know," cried Turi. "We must take them to the doctor at Syracuse, at once."

"In the back," said Orestes. "They'll be more comfortable. There are some empty sacks."

Antonio and Turi lifted the two into the back and jumped in themselves with Tom. Orestes took the wheel, turned the truck around and drove off toward Syracuse as fast as he could. Giangi had come to again and seemed a little better. He felt his head from time to time and said he'd been hit there. But Rags was crying and complaining about his right leg, which hung limp.

"Who hit you?" asked Turi, with Giangi in his arms.

"I don't know," the little boy said.

"Does your leg hurt?" Antonio asked Rags, whose head was in his lap. A lift of the chin and a groan were the only answer.

"What happened?"

"Those rats, those pigs, it was them," Rags managed to say. Then he spat over the side in disgust. He started to cry again.

That shook Turi. "The Burrosos?" he asked.

"Them," said Rags.

The cowards! The cowards! To take their revenge

on the children! They knew how much he cared for
them.

"But how? Did they beat you up?"

Rags shook his head.

"The truck, the truck was coming right on top of
me!" screamed Giangi suddenly. He clutched at Turi
and burst into tears.

The Burrosos' delivery truck, obviously. Turi shud-
dered and cold sweat broke out on his forehead again.
To drive a truck at a child! And all because he, Turi,
had refused to give in to their cheating and bullying.

"And then?" he demanded.

"Rags gave me a push and I fell," Giangi said.

Rags had kept his word. He had indeed looked after Giangi. He had saved his life. Turi reconstructed the scene for himself. The children and the dog were walking peacefully along the edge of the road. Suddenly the Burrosos' truck appeared from the opposite direction and swung straight across at Giangi. Rags realized the danger and hurled Giangi to one side, sending him rolling into the ditch where his head hit against something. But Rags himself was hit by the truck and knocked down, breaking a leg. Poor old Rags! And Tom had run to fetch Turi.

At Syracuse they stopped in front of Dr. Castrovilla's house. The office was closed at that hour, but the doctor opened it and they put Rags down on the couch. He was moaning and his teeth were clenched.

Giangi was lucky; he was fine and seemed completely recovered. A large bump was showing up on his head; but although it swelled bigger and bigger every minute, the more it swelled the better he looked. Turi sent him off with Antonio and Orestes to have a look around Syracuse.

When the doctor had examined Rags he had Turi help him prepare the plaster cast for the right leg. The boy must have been hit hard in the chest also, for he said it hurt, but luckily no ribs were broken.

"As long as no complications develop in his lungs, I don't think we need worry," the doctor said. "Take off his shorts."

Turi went over and tried to ease off Rags' shorts; the boy stopped him. His hand was shaking with pain, but he felt in his pocket and very, very carefully he pulled out his pink shell. He looked at it. It was in one piece. It glowed in the strong light which hung over the doctor's couch.

Outside, along the seafront where the boats were moored and where the tourist hotels were, Giangi stood between Orestes and Antonio. He was delightedly watching a fireworks display; but now and then he would ask anxiously about what was happening to Rags.

CHAPTER ELEVEN

Rags Comes Out of His Shell

It was now the end of October. One month after the grape harvest, one month after Rags' and Giangi's accident. The tomatoes were stored in oil, all ready for the winter, and smelling as sweet as summer. It was a beautiful, truly Sicilian October.

Rags sat in the doorway of Turi's cottage, his plaster cast resting on a stool. He was holding a little book of music. Those oval black marks climbing up and down the five lines, and sometimes linked together with little bars, now meant "music" to Rags. They were tunes and rhythms; they reminded him of the wind on the sea; they really meant something to him. Rags was a bright boy.

That very day they were going to cut away the plaster cast and bring out his newly healed leg, rather like

peeling the skin off a piece of fruit. During his illness
and his stay with Turi and Giangi—for they had taken
him home with them—Rags too had come all the way
out of the horrid bitter shell which his unhappiness
and loneliness had built up around him. He was really
a nice, friendly eight-year-old boy.

He and Giangi, who was only five years old, had
been making great progress with their lessons. Tufty
had been helping them. He had suddenly turned
schoolmaster, and seemed to have a natural bent for
teaching.

The little group was more united than ever. Each of
the five children was, in his own way, completely devoted to Turi. It wasn't as if he made any special effort
to win their affection; he was just himself. That was
why they loved him so much. No one had tried to
make them. They simply loved him for what he was.

They were happy to spend even a few minutes with
him, because he understood them so well. Perhaps the
reason was that Turi, although he *was* a grown-up,
was still in lots of ways a child inside.

Then, of course, they all shared their passion for
music. Besides learning to read and write for the first
time in his life, Rags was also learning to play the
mouth organ.

He was always a little breathless, poor boy, since
he had to stay sitting down with his right leg sheathed

in plaster, but he put such heart into his playing that he had really done wonders. Turi was very pleased with him. Of course he now had regular meals, which made a difference.

After that hideous September evening when Turi had carried Rags back to the cottage encased in plaster, and laid him to sleep in his own bed, Turi had not had the heart to take him back to the awful hovel where he used to live. The boy had been feverish for several days, though luckily he had not developed pneumonia.

Turi had gone to see Rags' parents the day after he was hurt; he told them about the accident and that Rags was staying with him. They had been very unpleasant to him, cursing their rebellious boy who did not want to go out and beg like their other sons. The mother had turned her back on Turi and just shuffled away in her broken-down slippers.

The father had sat gazing at Turi in a sort of stupor, dumb with wine or senility, or a combination of both. Turi was so angered that he went and shook him. He had heard that a job might be open in Antonio's father's fishing boat and he suggested this. The old man just stared blankly, without understanding at all. Then he lifted his fist and banged it down on the table. He sat obstinately, as if he were waiting for something to happen. Of course nothing would; even if it did, it wouldn't make any difference.

Turi escaped as quickly as he could, with the hoarse shouts of Rags' mother ringing in his ears.

On the way home he made up his mind to take the place in Antonio's father's boat himself, if Signor Messina would have him. He would have to work twice as hard now that he had two children to feed, and he must really build Rags up; there was still a danger that he might catch pneumonia.

So Turi worked twice as hard. Kind Dr. Castrovilla refused to accept anything for treating Rags. And today, the thirty-first of October, Orestes was taking Rags to Syracuse to have the plaster removed.

"I'm setting you free in time for the Spirits," the doctor said, massaging Rags' leg to get the circulation going faster and helping him to move it, which was difficult after the long period of inactivity.

"Will they be coming to your house?"

"Of course," said Giangi.

Rags looked at him hopefully.

"They'll bring presents," shouted Giangi, clapping his hands. "Oranges and dried figs."

"Perhaps they'll bring something else, too," said the doctor, winking at Turi.

In the next room there were two beautiful puppets with armor made out of old tomato cans, shields and swords and helmets. One was Rinaldo and the other was Orlando.

The following evening, Giangi and Rags put their

shoes—the only pair they owned between them—by the fireplace. During the night the Spirits would make themselves as small as ants, and creep through the cracks around the doors and windows to leave their presents.

On the morning of the second of November the shoes were indeed filled with dried figs, almonds, four oranges and the two puppets.

The two boys were speechless at the sight of so

many treasures. They picked up the two puppets very carefully by the rods that controlled them and placed them face to face. Strings were attached to their arms, and if you worked them cleverly you could make the warriors grasp their swords, pull them from the scabbards and hold them, poised for a fight.

Right in the middle of a fierce battle between Orlando and Rinaldo, the Spirits brought something for Turi, too—a letter.

It was an invitation to go to Rome and take the entrance examination for the Course of Musical Instruction for Bandmasters.

CHAPTER TWELVE

Departure

THOSE WERE CERTAINLY among the worst days of
Turi's life. Worse than when he had suddenly been
left alone in the world; worse than when he had realized his responsibility for Giangi and, later, Rags;
worse even than when he had found them both unconscious in the road and feared they might be dead.

Turi was waiting for the results of his examinations.
They had been held in Rome, in a great ugly building
full of school benches and people like himself from all
over Italy and professors who stared at him suspiciously. Turi had seen nothing of Rome apart from this.
He could not even remember what he had written or
how he had managed to answer those fiendish men
who had interviewed him. Everything he had worked
so hard to learn in the last few months seemed to melt

away into thin air. They had made him play his clarinet, too.

The suspense was almost unbearable. Of course it was unlikely that he would be accepted. He brushed away any hope as if it were an irritating fly.

But if he *did* win, what would he do with Giangi and Rags? Not for anything in the world would he be separated from Giangi, and he hated the thought of leaving Rags. To take one child to a huge strange city was a big enough risk; two would be quite impossible.

He had talked the problem over with Orestes, who had promised that he would look after Rags. This would at least ensure that he would not have to go back to the terrible life he had lived before. It was a solution, but it didn't make Turi any happier.

One moment Turi would be trying to crush his hopes; the next he would be trying to brush aside these depressing problems. He was a mixture of joy and despair, hope and anxiety.

Time is a strange thing; it can seem terribly long and terribly short. Sometimes years will fly by and sometimes minutes will drag on forever.

They were shaking the olives from the trees when the letter arrived. Giangi, Tom, and Rags ran to deliver it to Turi. He was working in the groves.

Turi straightened his back, which had been bent double as he gathered the tiny olives—hard now, but full of golden oil when crushed in the press—and looked at the little trio standing expectantly in front of him. Then he opened the letter.

He had been accepted.

Turi was one of the winners of the scholarship competition; the course of instruction would be held in Milan. Turi would have to leave.

"I've won!" he said, and suddenly his heart sank. All at once the leaves of the trees above his head were infinitely beautiful and the olives all around him on the soft ground seemed infinitely precious.

Giangi, Tom and Rags were stunned. Turi was going away. Would he take them? Silently they helped him put the olives into baskets. How could a marvelous dream turn out so sadly?

Antonio, Rosalia and Tufty cried, too. They turned their heads away and refused to look him in the eye. Their world seemed to be falling in pieces.

Turi scraped together his meager savings, collected the last wages due him, and even went so far as to sell his bed, his mattress and cooking pots so that he should not be completely penniless when he arrived in Milan in midwinter. He was terrified at the thought of Giangi; he didn't even have a coat. In Sicily a jacket and a scarf were enough. He did not mind for himself, but he must see that the child was properly clothed. He began to panic.

He was on the point of refusing to go.

Rags told him that at the dockyard, down near Cassibile, where they were building an oil refinery, they were looking for strong men to unload the trucks, and were offering good pay. Did Rags realize that he could not come with them? Turi had not had the courage to say anything to him. He seemed perfectly calm. Sometimes Turi would look at him and wonder. What was he thinking about? What was going on behind those dark eyes?

Rags kept silent.

But when Turi unwrapped a parcel on the table and drew out a new overcoat and put it on Giangi, Rags suddenly burst into tears and ran to hide in a corner with his face against the wall. Tom ran over to comfort him, and then he cried and cried into the dog's black fur. He cried as he had never cried before.

Turi let him alone. When he calmed down Turi went and explained that he would not be leaving Rags alone for long, that he would be back soon, very soon, and with a good job that would help him keep Rags with him for always.

Rags and Giangi went out with Tom to show off the new coat.

Left alone, Turi sat down on the one remaining chair and looked around him. He had made up his mind to go. Heaven only knew what he would find in that cold northern city; he pictured it at the very top of the world, on the summit of a high frozen mountain covered with ice and snow.

Orestes loaded them all onto his truck, including Antonio, Tufty and Rosalia with their instruments. They wanted—so they said—to play a little tune in Turi's honor before the train left.

Turi and Giangi did not have much luggage; their possessions were few. Tom carried all his on his back!

Not many people were leaving Syracuse that night. A strong wind was blowing and bending the palm trees over into the station yard. Lights dotted at intervals along the roof of the shed lit up the platform, which seemed to stretch forever.

Everyone stared at the strange little group—a man, a hunchback, five children and a dog—making its way toward the Syracuse–Rome train. Their amazement grew when, after Turi, Giangi and Tom were settled in an empty compartment, the children left on the platform took out their instruments and began to play. Rosalia sang:

> "People who come to Sicily
>   Gaze on it in delight,
>   Swear they've never seen anywhere
>   An island half so bright.
>   The Golden Shell gleams in the sun.
>   Mt. Etna laughs beneath the snows.

Our lighthouse throws its beam afar.
And Anopo's waters flow,
And Anopo's waters flow."

Time went by, and still the train did not leave. Orestes went to ask the stationmaster the cause of the delay. He was told not to worry; a freight train loaded with oranges had to leave before the passenger train could go. There is always time for passengers, but if oranges are kept waiting they go bad.

Orestes went back to the train where Turi, leaning out of the window, asked anxiously if he had seen Rags and the others. They had drifted away, saying that they were going to look for Orestes. But Orestes had seen nobody. Turi was worried, especially about Rags, and begged Orestes to see that he came to no harm. The hunchback promised once again to take good care of him.

"Say good-bye to Antonio and Rosalia and Tufty for me," called Turi as the train finally began to move. Orestes stood all alone in the middle of the platform, waving.

The little points of light faded away into the distance; the three travelers sped off into the unknown, with night falling all around them.

Rags' disappearance troubled Turi. Had he really not wanted to say good-bye?

Already they were passing through gray Catania, its

elegant, rich houses with their wide balconies hidden in the darkness. Turi's thoughts kept turning to Rags. He was thinking about him so intensely that he could almost see him.

He looked up and his eyes met Rags', deep and dark, watching him from behind the glass of the window onto the corridor. Was it an hallucination? Imagination? Turi looked across at Giangi, who was fast asleep, hugging his dog. Tom wasn't asleep; his ears were pricked, his nose was twitching and, although he was keeping quite still so as not to wake Giangi, his whole body was straining toward the corridor. Turi was suddenly quite certain that Rags was actually on the train.

He flung himself into the corridor. "What are you doing here?" Syracuse was far away, Marzamemi even farther. The train was running along the dark coastline.

"What are you doing here?" Turi's voice barely concealed his joy, his absurd feeling of relief. It was enough for Rags. "Antonio paid for the ticket," he said, gesturing vaguely behind him.

Turi was dumbfounded. What could Rags do in Milan? Suddenly he thought of shoes. Rags didn't have any and it would be very cold in Milan. He looked down at Rags' feet; he was wearing a pair of women's shoes, far too big for him. Heavens above, where had he got hold of those?

Turi passed his hand across his forehead. Rags, un-daunted, stood planted in the middle of the corridor, his hands plunged into his jacket pockets, a scarf pulled right up over his nose and a crumpled old cap pulled down over his ears, all ready to face the rigors of a northern winter. He gestured behind him again.

"Antonio bought the tickets."

"So I gathered," said Turi, drawing the boy toward him. He gave a resigned shrug. He felt foolishly happy.

Then the unbelievable happened. Rags took Turi by the hand and led him along the corridor. "They're here. All of them." All? What did he mean? In the next car, curled up in the corner of a compartment, were Antonio, Tufty and Rosalia.

Turi's blood ran cold. He flung open the door. "What are you doing here? What are you doing here?" Poor Turi couldn't think of anything else to say; he was speechless.

"We've got tickets!" cried Tufty triumphantly, wav-ing them in the dim light.

"And our instruments, too," added Rosalia. She was wrapped in an enormous black shawl which covered her from head to toe. On the luggage rack lay the guitar, the accordion and the tambourine.

A mist floated before Turi's eyes and he sat down or, rather, collapsed onto a seat. The children crowded around him.

"Turi, we're coming with you." "To Milan." "We won't let you go alone."

"You are all getting out at the next station and taking the first train back to Pachino," Turi managed to say. At once their expressions changed; they became obstinate.

"We're coming with you." It was Antonio.

"What shall I do? How can I take you with me? Have you thought of all the difficulties I'm facing as it is? If you all come I can't possibly support you."

"We will look after ourselves," said Antonio.

"But what do you think you are going to do in a big city like Milan? No one will employ babies like you. And what will your parents say?"

They all shrugged. They would rather be with Turi. Only Rosalia looked doubtful for a moment. Turi took her by the shoulders.

"Rosalia, you want to go home, don't you? Isn't it true you would like to go back?"

Rosalia was on the verge of tears. "My sister is married now."

Turi played his last card. He was sick at heart.

"Children. I haven't any money. Be good and listen to me. If you won't get out at the next station and go home, remember what I am telling you now. When we reach Milan you will have to look after yourselves." He looked at them one by one. They were too young to understand and all looked cheerfully back at him.

"Or else I shall hand you over to the police and have you sent home whether you like it or not," finished Turi.

What sort of talk was this? He should have called the guard immediately, explained the situation and sent them all home then and there. Why didn't he do it now? That would have been the logical, sensible, grown-up thing to do. But Turi was not completely grown-up. He knew only too well that any such sensible action would rob him forever of the trust and affection of these four children, who were so determined not to leave him. To do such a thing was beyond him.

"Have you had anything to eat?" he asked, feeling suddenly very tired as he thought of the responsibility of all that trust and affection.

"Rosalia has brought some bread." Tufty had a sausage which had been spirited out of his mother's kitchen, and Antonio had some bread too. They had even thought of food—what perfect organization!

Together they returned to Turi's compartment, where Giangi lay sleeping. Tom wagged his tail with joy, gently so as not to disturb his friend. Soon they all fell asleep.

Only Turi, his eyes wide open, saw coming toward them, looming ever larger, higher and more menacing, the gigantic frozen mountain, covered with ice and snow.

Part
Two

CHAPTER ONE

The Caretaker at Number 15

It was morning and yet it was still dark. They had had to spend hours and hours on the hard benches of the station waiting room. The cold prodded them with sly, icy fingers. It crept in, not only under their clothes but under their very skin. They felt as though they would never be warm again.

The houses were so tall they looked like mountains; they seemed to reach right up to the sky. It was terrifying. The lighted windows were like gleaming eyes, staring into space.

More gleaming eyes, noisy ones this time, passed close to the children, who drew back in terror. Then finally, in the murk, they saw a familiar sight—the friendly steamy breath of a horse pulling a cab. It was the only one, perhaps the last.

Turi asked the cabman a question. They spoke two completely different languages and could hardly understand each other, but in the end Turi found out which way to go.

They came to the outskirts of the city. The sky—no, you couldn't see the sky—the air, then, was slowly getting a little lighter, but it became no clearer, for it was heavy with thick, gray fog. The huge plane trees along the streets where the streetcars were clattering looked like poles topped with clusters of gray, artificial leaves, not like real trees at all.

A siren made the children jump, and a swarm of men and women in overalls came bicycling around the corner of a building. They all went into the building, which had countless tiny windows, and disappeared. The siren gave a second, satisfied-sounding wail. Other sirens took up the cry and it suddenly seemed as if the gray blanket enshrouding the city were about to press down and suffocate them. Towering chimneys, factories, engines, bicycle wheels, the monotonous grind of machines—they closed in on Turi and the children, driving them onward, like fugitives, into the wintry morning.

"What, doesn't he live here anymore?" "No, he has gone to Sesto, to be near the factory." "Sesto? Where's that?" "Not far, but you'll have to take a train."

The one and only person who could have helped

them, spoken their language, had gone away. Even he had been lured away by some noisy machine. Turi had vaguely remembered the face of the fellow Sicilian whom he had hoped to find here, but now it faded completely, leaving him alone again, in the cold.

The building where the course of instruction for bandmasters was to be held was red brick. Inside were dirty, dank corridors and attendants who were either unfriendly or else just not at their shabby desks. It was all very depressing. As it was Sunday, Turi could not find anyone to help; everything was shut and deserted.

They started walking again.

Signora Pierina Cente was busily sweeping the sidewalk in front of the apartment building of which she was caretaker, and grumbling about the dogs that dirty the corners of doorways.

"Good morning, Signor Keller."

"Good morning, Pierina. Working so early?"

"Well, I like that! I've washed all the stairs already. Down on my knees too, step by step. Your shirts are ironed, too. I have them ready."

"They're done already?"

"What should I be hanging about for? Today I have to do ten for Signor Manzani and five for Signor Quarti. They must be ready by tonight."

"Have a good day, Pierina!"

"Good morning, Signor Keller."

And she went back to work, sweeping more energetically than ever.

A little black and white snout poked out from the doorway, and was greeted with a loud scolding from Signora Pierina. "What are you up to, Missi? Down to the cellar at once, do you understand? Off you go!" She stood with one arm pointing down the steps, the other resting on her broom handle. The little cat did an about turn, and with the most dignified air possible, retraced its steps.

Just then, a strange party—a man carrying a suitcase, five children and a dog—rounded the corner of the street. The dog was immediately singled out by the caretaker as a personal enemy. The piece of pavement outside Number 15 of a certain Milanese street, not far from the Square of the Five Days, belonged to her, and let anyone who tried to challenge her beware. To her, dogs spelled trouble, and she prepared to take a firm stand. But, to her great astonishment, this dog showed no desire to provoke her; it seemed an intelligent, well-behaved animal.

The man and the children were walking slowly, looking about them as they went, as if they were strangers searching for something.

The caretaker watched them curiously. She noticed that the children's clothes were not nearly warm enough to protect them against the cold of a city like Milan. But this was no concern of hers. And, realizing she had been staring at them, she returned to her sweeping with slightly exaggerated enthusiasm.

Instead, it was Turi who approached her and asked if by any chance she could tell him of anyone who might have a room to let. What on earth is the fellow talking about? wondered Signora Pierina. Turi's strange accent sounded to her almost like a foreign language.

"What should I know about rooms to let?" she said in her own dialect as a sort of reaction to the strangeness of Turi's voice. "I don't know anything about rooms." She started sweeping again. They must be hungry, those children. They had that look on their faces. She had been a children's nurse and knew the signs.

"We are from Sicily and don't know anything about Milan." Turi was almost overcome by tiredness, from the dreadfully long journey and worry about the children.

Signora Pierina suddenly stopped sweeping and looked up. "From Sicily?"

"We're from Marzamemi, near Syracuse." Turi didn't know why he was telling her this. Perhaps because he couldn't stop thinking about the great distance they had come, and how ridiculous it all seemed.

"And you're wandering around looking for a room with all these children? Are you crazy?"

Turi threw up his hands despairingly.

"Leave them with me while you see what you can do."

Turi stood and stared at the woman. She finished sweeping the last patch of sidewalk, and made her way inside. "Come along, come along. I've no time to waste." She clearly meant what she said. Rags and Giangi moved after her and the others followed.

Turi put the suitcase down in a corner. The five children huddled together and said nothing. Signora Pierina took a bottle from a cupboard in her spotless kitchen, filled a small glass, and offered it to Turi. "Drink this." It was brandy.

"I won a contest to become a bandmaster," explained Turi. "The course begins tomorrow and if I don't find somewhere to stay today I just don't know what I shall do."

"Are these all your children?"

"Not one of them."

The woman shook her head in bewilderment. Well, the children could wait here where it was warm. Turi thanked her and went out.

For a moment Signora Pierina seemed lost in thought; then she began to scold the children.

"What do you think you are doing standing there like so many stuffed dummies! Come over here."

She took off their coats and scarves, examining them one by one and shaking her head disapprovingly.

Then she made them all sit down at the table and she lit the stove. In a few minutes each of them had a big bowl of milky coffee. She rummaged in the cupboard drawers and brought out some bread.

"Eat up. Go on, dip the bread in the coffee. It's yesterday's, but older bread is better for your stomachs—it's lighter."

Tom, huddled against Giangi's chair, was resting his nose on the boy's knee. Giangi surreptitiously passed him a little bread. Tom began crunching it noisily. This gave the game away.

"Go and eat out of Missi's dish, you. Go on!"

Tom hesitated. The cat might not think this a good idea. And anyway the dish was empty.

Signora Pierina put some bread and milk in the bowl and sent the cat down to the cellar. Then she hustled Tom over and told him to start eating; he didn't need to be told twice.

Giangi could hardly keep his eyes open, with all that hot milk inside him. All the children had flushed cheeks. Weariness was gradually overcoming them. It crept under their skin, oozed through their very pores and settled on their limbs like a heavy blanket.

This did not escape Signora Pierina. She knew all about children, and these were tired out.

"Come along, bedtime now."

Giangi almost fell out of his chair. Signora Pierina

130

picked him up under her arm. "Come along, now." Rags took her other hand.

While she was preparing the beds, Giangi and Rags stood in front of a chest of drawers, staring blearily at a framed photograph of a young man in soldier's uniform.

"Hurry up, I don't have all day!" Signora Pierina picked Giangi up again and was about to put him into bed when he pointed at the photograph, and said, "That's Turi." Rags nodded.

The woman stopped for a moment, surprised. Then she hugged Giangi and kissed him. "No, pet, that's not Turi. It's Lino, my son. He was killed in the war."

Giangi looked at her blankly. "Turi," he repeated, and fell asleep the moment his head touched the pillow. Rags climbed up next to him and the woman tucked them in. Then she settled Tufty and Rosalia in the next bed.

She turned and looked at them as she went out of the room. For a moment Giangi looked like her own little son whom she had had to leave behind when she went out to take care of other people's children. Then for an instant she saw him as a baby girl whom she had nursed and brought up and loved like a daughter; and then he reminded her of Signor Keller's children, who lived above her and whom she had watched grow up.

Antonio was playing the strong man. Tired? Not he!
He didn't want to sleep. But the caretaker put up a
camp bed for him in a corner of the kitchen, out of the
way, and made him lie down. She sent Tom down to
the cellar to keep the cat company, locked the door
and went off to do her shopping.

When she returned she washed fifteen shirts and
hung them up in the kitchen near the stove.

When Turi came back at about one o'clock, he
found the children sitting around a bowl of lovely,
steaming minestrone. They were staring at it wide-
eyed. They had never seen or tasted anything like it
before.

"I thought you were never coming back!" exclaimed
Pierina to Turi.

"I came to take the children out for something to
eat."

"Goodness me, what time do you eat in your part of
the world? It's late, you know."

Turi looked at her in surprise.

"I said it's late. Come along, sit down and eat.
There's plenty of minestrone for all of us."

It tasted delicious.

"Here, try some cheese from my own village. Do
you like it?"

Giangi nodded, his mouth full.

"Pet!" she cried, giving him a smacking kiss which
almost made him choke.

Turi had had no luck. Many places refused to accept him; they did not take children, they did not take dogs.

Turi was frantic. "Whatever shall I do?" he kept repeating.

"Cheer up, you're sure to find something. Ask the caretakers, they know everything that goes on. Come on now, don't give up. 'Where there's a will there's a way'!"

With this parting shot, Signora Pierina disappeared to go and wash up for Signora Keller, who was temporarily without any domestic help.

Turi went out again, feeling very despondent. But when he returned, toward evening, he had found a place to stay.

The caretaker greeted him. "That Rosalia is such a good girl. Do you know, she washed all the dishes for me and swept the kitchen?" She was as proud as if Rosalia were her own daughter. "I'm all alone here. Would you like to leave her with me for a while? She could look after the entrance when I have to go out."

She was on her tenth shirt. Putting down the iron, she took off her glasses for a moment to rub her eyes and, hands on hips, waited for his reply.

"You are very kind," Turi said.

"Well, what about it?"

"I must admit it would just about save my life if you could look after her."

"You will be responsible for her, won't you? I don't want any trouble."

She looked anxiously at Turi, and then she smiled. No, there would not be any trouble. She understood all about children and their faces couldn't hide much from her.

CHAPTER TWO

The Grand Department Store

THE CITY WAS PAVED with a hard, black crust, which completely hid the earth. And real earth was so scarce that they surrounded it with concrete and sowed it with thin, sickly grass. They closed it in with iron railings and at night they locked it up for fear someone should steal it away.

Oh, for the hills and the sea!

The sea washes and cleanses; things never get really dirty by the sea. But the city was far from the sea and it was dirty all the time. It was dirty even though they tried to make it seem clean by festooning it with lights. The lights were red and green and yellow and blue. Some flashed on and off, some shone steadily, and they went on and on until it was impossible to see where they could ever end.

Giangi and Rags would stand with upturned faces for hours, just watching the lights. They could never understand just how and where they went; or how and why they made so many beautiful patterns as they hung in the huge darkness on the face of some great building, or floated high in the starless sky.

The lights on the great Christmas tree in the middle of the square were somehow even more astonishing. Giangi and Rags had never seen a Christmas tree before; they thought it magical.

Then there were the lights in the shop windows. These were lights that positively made them feel warm and good.

Perfume and music drifted out through the glass doors of the Grand Department Store. Giangi and Rags had been standing against the side of the Cathedral for hours, staring at the store; suddenly, without really intending it, they found themselves in the doorway. They stopped, dazzled; the place was a blaze of light.

The thronging customers were gesturing, pointing, examining and buying things; the assistants were gesturing, pointing, and urging customers to try things. Then they wrapped them in bags and packages. They might have been robots.

There were boxes of toffee, chocolates, candied chestnuts, little net bags full of golden chocolate money—good to eat, but no good to pay with. For that you need real money, which is not made of gold but of dirty paper.

There were colored scarves. Rows of umbrellas with hard, straight, imperious handles, or with curving, dejected handles, their heads looking almost too heavy for their long necks. Soft gloves, with fingers spread out as if they were already on a hand, and lined inside with lambskin or rabbit fur to keep out the cold.

Whose was that enormous glove hanging up there just above the counter, with its fingers poised to grab something? Perhaps it belonged to some enormous giant who would suddenly decide to pounce on Rags and Giangi and Tom and demand to know what they were doing there. They had better get out quickly— that glove must have belonged to the biggest giant in the world.

There was a staircase that stood still and moved at the same time. People stayed quite still on it and yet they moved upward. Giangi and Rags thought it was very clever indeed; but the people using it didn't seem very satisfied—they kept looking around distractedly and glancing at their watches. They obviously thought the staircase didn't go fast enough.

On the floor above, there were more things for sale. These were the best. There were wooden horses to ride, toy cars that looked just like real ones, with brakes, a steering wheel, a horn, and a license plate so that you could tell who the owner was in case he broke the law. There were dolls that looked like little girls, with soft hair and clothes in the latest styles. One was sitting under an electric hair dryer with her hair in curlers!

Tom suddenly found himself face to face with a motionless image of himself; its glassy eyes were gazing fixedly into his own.

Tom sniffed at it nervously. How odd. It smelled of mothballs and powder. Tom sneezed. It couldn't really be a poodle; it must be some other sort of dog.

People were also squeezing themselves into a mechanical box which went up and down. On each floor it spilled some people out and let others in. It did this over and over again.

On still another floor, the crowds were having a rest and drinking cups of hot chocolate with whipped cream. The floating mounds of cream would slowly spread out and become streaked with chocolate; how strange this mixture of hot and cold, sweet and bitter, must taste.

On the top floor of the Grand Store were whole rooms, with modern furniture, American-style kitchens, chairs, beds, lamps, desks. Everything was placed just as it would be in a real house.

The customers bought and bought, but the Grand

Store never ran out of goods. The shelves were always full; replacements arrived as if by magic. A bell rang through the store. The sound echoed shrilly down the stairs, came out of the elevators, reached the glass doors and bounced back in.

A voice from nowhere announced: "Our customers are kindly requested to hurry. The Grand Store will close in ten minutes."

The music ended suddenly, and the giant hive stopped humming.

"Run along now, children. We're closing."

Ten minutes, ten minutes, ten minutes. Everyone packed up hurriedly; their very movements seemed to echo the words.

"Will our customers please make their way toward the exits. The Grand Store will close in five minutes."

The clerks took off their white overalls and put on their jackets. They suddenly seemed small and tired.

The blinds came down over the glass doors and behind, inside the store, peace and order reigned. The moving stairs came slowly to rest. The lights went out.

Closed. It was tight closed. Even the service doors were shut, after the shopgirls and clerks and delivery boys had left.

Very, very slowly the doors of a large kitchen cabinet in one of the American kitchens swung open. Curled up inside was Rags.

He slid out, trying not to rattle the dummy bottles and the pots and pans. Tom whined softly. The doors of a gleaming broom cupboard moved apart, and out scrambled Giangi and Tom, who was all muzzled up in a scarf.

The neon lights flashed their shafts of light through the long gallery of windows. Red, yellow, blue.

Stealthily the three crept downstairs. Tom's nails clicked and skidded on the motionless steps of the escalator. "Shhh!"

The lighted shop windows on the ground floor and the illuminated signs outside sent brilliant flashes right up to the windows of the toy department.

"Toys."

The word wasn't spelled out in neon letters, but they loomed enormous in Giangi's and Rags' imagination.

For them the toys were far more than mere playthings; they were something real, something important. Even the Spirits, squeezing like ants under the doors, could surely never bring such wonderful things. How would they get them inside? And also, the Spirits of Marzamemi were almost certainly much poorer than the Spirits of Milan. They could never have afforded the marvels to be found in the Grand Department Store.

Rags, seated in a jeep, worked the pedals and drove

carefully around the shining wooden floor. Giangi rode a red tricycle. Tom, still muzzled, ran frantically from one to the other. Without a word Rags untied the scarf and Giangi explained with his hands that there would be trouble if he made a sound. Luckily he was a clever dog and understood. He sat down among his woolly friends and kept so quiet that he could have been a toy, too.

They stroked the toys. They gazed at them. They couldn't have enough of them. They longed to have them for their own—well, one at least. That would have been something.

Outside, the neon lights were dimmed. The windows were dark. In the black depths within, Giangi and Rags had fallen asleep, clinging to the tricycle and the jeep. All at once there was a noise. It was so steady, so regular, that it was hardly noticeable. Tom pricked up his ears and came to life among the motionless poodles.

CHAPTER THREE

Thieves

THREE SHAFTS OF LIGHT searched this way and that. They halted, went out and then shone bright again. The noise had stopped. Behind the beams of the flashlights all was frighteningly quiet.

At last the three beams found the stairs and began to climb up. Then Tom barked.

He barked loudly and urgently.

Suddenly the service lights went on. The night watchmen, revolvers in hand, rushed out in alarm.

The flashlights immediately went out.

Who was there, behind those three shafts of light?

Rags pressed his face to the railings of the first-floor balcony, looked down and saw a shadow hidden behind one of the flashlights. He yelled, "There he is!"

It was the signal for action. The night watchmen hurled themselves down the stairs. One of the thieves fired. A watchman toppled over, wounded, and fell down the stairs, firing as he went.

Rags drew back, grabbed Giangi and hurriedly pushed him away from the railings. They found themselves in front of a small door. They opened it and there was a little room lined with levers, buttons, electric wires and knobs. A red light kept watch over it all.

Who can tell what passed through Rags' mind at that moment? On a sudden impulse he grasped the levers, one after another, and pulled.

Darkness, shots, shadows lurking behind beams of light, Tom barking like a mad thing. It seemed to Rags like the end of the world. It must be their punishment for being bad, for having deserted Turi.

He went on pulling the levers. Perhaps he hoped to blow the whole place up.

The lights went on. The moving staircase, whispering very softly, began to move. A disembodied voice cried out of nowhere: "The Grand Store will close in ten minutes." The elevator doors closed and the little metal boxes shot upward.

A fabulous electric train set off along its miniature tracks, threatening to run down a truck waiting at a crossing. A children's merry-go-round started turning frantically, the little seats twirling at the end of their chains, and the wooden horses rocking on their poles, their bridles dangling.

In the American kitchen in the window, a mechanical cook began to slice up a plastic sausage, opening his mouth in an inviting smile at the nonexistent passersby. A row of models, draped in furs, with faces like the loveliest film stars, paraded past. Up and down the red velvet gangway they went, trailing the skirts of their evening dresses, smiling brilliant, painted smiles.

A raucous, disjointed tune blared out. It was an absurd song, the latest hit. And through the music, within the glaringly lighted store, came the unmistakable sound of more gunshots.

One night watchman was blocking the service entrance, which had been forced open. Another, slumped on the moving staircase, kept ascending; his companions had not had time to remove him. The third had telephoned for the police and was now cautiously descending an emergency staircase to surprise the thieves from behind.

They were firing blindly in their panic.

Rags and Giangi, from their vantage point up in the balcony, saw the thief creeping behind the counters toward the watchman.

"Look out! Look out!" they yelled.

The music was playing madly; it was impossible to hear. The children ran along the railing.

Here stupid models were parading by. Giangi and Rags darted between them along the gangway. Giangi almost tripped over one; he clutched it, it stopped for a moment, tottering and smothering him in chiffon and pearls. Rags hurled himself against it and pushed. The model leaned over a little farther. Then Giangi turned and gave it a shove. It twisted around, fell heavily against the railing, paused an instant, and then crashed down onto the glove counter below and from there to the floor.

The crash made the watchman spin sharply around. And only just in time. He grasped the thief's gun arm and the shot went wide, right up in the air. Then the watchman hit him. They rolled over together on top of the model; her empty limbs fell apart.

At that moment police car sirens sounded in the street outside.

CHAPTER FOUR

Interrogation

"Send them in."

"Yes, sir."

"The dog, too?"

"The dog, too."

"What is your name?"

"Giangi."

"Giangi what?" Silence. "I asked you, what is your name?"

"Giangi."

"Yes, all right, but what else? Come now, who is your father?"

"Turi."

"Turi? And who is Turi?"

"Turi's just Turi."

"All right, we'll leave it at that. And you, what is your name?"

"Rags."

146

"Rags? What sort of a name is that?"

"Yes, he is called Rags, even if he doesn't wear them any more."

"Turi gave me some trousers with pockets in them."

"That's quite enough about Turi, whoever he may be. Are you his son too?"

Rags shook his head.

"I can't make any sense of all this."

"Excuse me, Inspector, but we seem to have a couple of cuckoos here."

"What? What? Must you stick your nose in too, Constable Sciminna? You'll only muddle things worse."

"No, Inspector, sir, excuse me for mentioning it, but you see these are Sicilian children."

"Ah. I see. Well, perhaps you *can* help me then."

"Cuckoo yourself," muttered Giangi, in the same dialect as the constable.

"May I ask what this word means?"

"It means 'stupid,' sir," said the constable, tapping his forehead with his finger.

"What were you doing in the Grand Store in the middle of the night?"

Giangi and Rags tilted their chins and did not answer.

"Excuse me, Inspector, I'm sorry, but the reporters and photographers are here."

"They can wait, they can wait. These two are driving me out of my mind. I am not to be disturbed during interrogation."

"Yes, but it's a little difficult to convince them. This is a big story, what with the children and the dog."

"Tell them to wait. And leave me in peace."

"Very good, Inspector."

"Now then. How did you get into the Grand Store?"

"We just went in," said Rags, shrugging his shoulders.

"Yes, but who *let* you in?"

"You're cuckoo, too," exclaimed Giangi.

"Now then, show a little respect, my boy."

"Take it easy, kids," said the constable in Sicilian dialect. "This is the Inspector."

"Come on now. Confess. The thieves made you go into the store and hide so that you could open the doors for them."

"I'm tired," Giangi said.

"What cunning! See how cleverly they avoid the questions!"

"Calm yourself, Inspector. May I question them?"

"All right, Constable. Go ahead. Just try it."

"Now listen, kids. We want to know how you came to be in the Grand Store in the middle of the night. All good children are in bed and asleep at that hour, aren't they?"

The two nodded. Good children are asleep then, and don't upset Turi.

"Turi!" cried Giangi, on the verge of tears.

"Turi will be so worried," murmured Rags.

"What are they saying?" asked the Inspector.

"I think they are saying that this Turi will be angry with them for being out so late at night," said the constable. Giangi and Rags nodded remorsefully.

"Well, why did you do it?" the constable asked patiently.

"It was the yellow chick!" Giangi burst out suddenly. The men looked at each other in bewilderment.

"Yes, the one in the blue egg!" put in Rags.

"It was pretty!"

"So the yellow chick made you go into the Grand Department Store? That's it! That's it! I told you so! It's some kind of password!" shouted the Inspector.

"I believe it's that advertisement that lights up in the Square," remarked the constable modestly.

"Where was this chick?"

"In the dark, high up," said Rags, flinging his arms wide to emphasize his point. Then he let them flop, and stood quite still.

"Pretty!" exclaimed Giangi again happily.

"Excuse me, Inspector. The journalists insist on seeing the boys and taking their photographs. Otherwise they will miss the morning editions."

"We've told them to leave us in peace. Let's have a

word with the night watchmen now. Bring them in," ordered the Inspector.

In came the watchmen from the Grand Store. Tom wagged his tail.

"They're friends," Rags said. Everyone looked at everyone else. The constable smiled, got a stern look, and pretended to be stroking his moustache.

"Andrea Brambilla and Antonio Bossi, you say in your statement that or your rounds of inspection you did not observe the presence of the children in the Grand Store."

"That is correct."

"It's lucky they were there. They saved our skins," said Brambilla.

"Now then, children. Where did you hide, and why?" demanded the Inspector.

"In the pots and pans," answered Rags at once.

Everyone laughed.

"*Where?*" asked the Inspector.

"In *with* the pots and pans," replied Rags, with a tired little shrug.

"Ah! Now I understand! This rascal hid himself in the cabinet in the American kitchen. Well, I never!" said one of the watchmen, in his strange northern dialect. Giangi and Rags looked at him in amazement.

"And you, where were you hiding?" they asked Giangi.

"Where the brooms were, and Tom sneezed. And I

tied my scarf around his mouth because he wanted to talk."

"He did talk later on, luckily for us," said Antonio Bossi. "If it hadn't been for him we should never have heard those crooks getting in, and that's for sure."

"Ah, it was he who gave the alarm?"

"Yes sir, that brave dog there. I bet he understands more than most humans."

"And may we ask just what you wanted to do in the Grand Store at that hour of the night?"

Explanations. How could they possibly explain things to other people when they didn't even know how to explain them to themselves?

"They wanted to play, that's all." The one watchman understood it all, only he spoke in such a funny way.

"How much did they give you? The thieves, how much did they give you to go in and open up for them? You might as well tell the truth, we know everything."

"Bang! Bang! They were shooting!" cried Giangi, still haunted by the flying shots. He had never quite lost the dim memory of other shots, long ago. Giangi was afraid. "Turi!" He burst into tears.

"Why don't you leave him alone? Can't you see he's dead tired, poor little guy?" said Andrea Brambilla.

"If they hadn't thrown Gina Lollobrigida on top of

me, I should be dead by now. They saved my life, that's all I know!"

"What? What? Lollobrigida?"

"Yes, we have a display of clothes on the balcony and the models are made up like movie stars. The model of La Lollo was the one the kids shoved over to warn Bossi that the thief was behind him."

"Excuse me, Inspector . . ."

"The reporters? I'll throw them all out, do you hear?"

"Yes, sir. But this time it's someone with a woman. He says they've been looking all around the police stations for two children and a dog, so I thought . . ."

"And so?"

"So perhaps these are the two they are looking for."

"Right. Bring them in."

The color came rushing back into Turi's face when he saw the two boys sitting there in front of the Inspector's desk. Signora Pierina burst into tears and hugged Giangi. Tom jumped around them like a mad thing.

"All right. Everything is settled. But don't you know you can't send two children around on their own like that with a dog without a muzzle? If it bites someone, then what do you do?"

"Tom doesn't bite," growled Giangi, offended.

"He'll bite you, you rat!" Rags said fiercely. The

constable grabbed him by the arm, clapped a hand over his mouth and looked around nervously.

"What did he say?" demanded the Inspector.

"I didn't quite catch it, sir," said the constable. Under his breath he hissed, "Shut up, you little fool, or they'll put you in jail!"

"There is a fine of five thousand lire for bringing a dog into the Grand Store without a muzzle."

Turi looked stunned. Five thousand lire! Just where would he find that sum?

"Couldn't you let them off, just this once? The dog has a muzzle and he is properly licensed. I can't think what's become of the muzzle, can you, Augusto?"

Rags pulled the muzzle from his pocket. "Here it is! Here's the muzzle! The dog does have a muzzle."

"He has one, but he's not wearing it. The fine is five thousand lire."

Turi's shoulders sagged, despondent.

Then Signora Pierina opened her wrinkled old bag and pulled out a green note. "I brought it along . . . one never knows," she said, almost apologetically.

When they left, the street lamps were still alight in the fog which shrouded the Cathedral Square.

CHAPTER FIVE

Tufty in Business

TUFTY HAD STATIONED HIMSELF at the corner of the school and was waiting for the boys to come out.

They came at last, scuffing their feet, hitting each other with book bags and waving rulers in each other's faces.

"That was a horrible problem we had today," two boys were saying as they walked toward him, exercise books open in their hands, bags on their shoulders.

"The homework's even worse!"

"How much will you pay me if I give you the right answer now?" Tufty demanded suddenly, walking up to them.

"Which class are you in?"

"Third," answered Tufty, thinking to himself, Saint Rosalia, forgive me for this lie.

"Will you do this whole problem for me, and show me how to work it out, too?"

"Of course."

"But how do I know it will be right?"

"I'm in the third class, so I've already done all those questions."

The boy felt in his pockets.

"I'll give you fifty lire."

"That's not enough. You'll let him copy it." Tufty indicated the other boy. "I'm not doing two people's work for half price."

The two looked at each other.

"This is all I've got. How about you?"

The other boy dug some ten-lire coins out of his pocket. He added them up. Sixty lire. "I can give you fifty lire, too. That will make a hundred."

"O.K. then. Hand it over."

Tufty rested the book on his schoolbag. He licked the much-licked pencil they lent him and solved the problem with careless ease. He pocketed the hundred lire and walked along to another corner of the huge school building, which filled a whole block.

In a quarter of an hour he had written an essay on "The Most Wonderful Memory of My Life," and earned another hundred lire. The essay was more difficult than the problem. Anyway, who cared what the most wonderful memory of that dope was? It had taken a good deal of imagination to dream something up.

156

If only Tufty had been able to enroll in a school, he could have done three times as much business, with all his schoolmates as customers. As things were, while he was doing problems for one boy he was losing the chance of an essay for someone else, and vice versa.

Giuseppangelo Baroni, known as Tufty, had one great quality in his favor: he never gave up.

With the first hundred lire he went straight to a stationer's and bought a pad of writing paper, an envelope, a pen and a stamp. One thing was certain; when Tufty got down to correspondence, it always had something to do with a brilliant idea involving his godfather, Giuseppangelo Castronuovo.

Respected godfather, Tufty began, the tip of his tongue sticking out as usual. He was sitting in a corner of the caretaker's room at Number 15. Rosalia was sewing a hem as she kept an eye on the people who came in and out of the building. It was she who had asked him in.

This letter comes to bring you my respectful greetings and to say that I am in good health and hope you are likewise.

New paragraph. *Finding myself in Milan on business . . .* This was rather a bold statement, but after all, that very morning he had concluded deals worth two hundred lire. A regular commercial undertaking. Trade.

Finding myself in Milan on business, I have not been able to continue with my studies at school in Syracuse, as it would be too far to travel every day. I should think so! More than nine hundred miles! It seemed an excellent reason.

I could go to school in Milan only I don't have the money for the fees. I expect you will be displeased if your godson cannot finish his education as well as he would have done in Syracuse.

"What's he writing?" asked Signora Pierina, making Tufty jump. He was deep in his letter.

"I'm writing to my godfather so that he'll send me to school here in Milan."

"Ah, he's a real bookworm, this boy!"

The caretaker hurried off again. She was carrying a huge basket of wet clothes to hang out in the yard.

Tufty reread the last sentence. What must his godfather have said when he learned that Giuseppangelo Baroni had simply dropped everything and removed himself to Milan "on business"? Italiano Baroni had already sent letters full of furious protests, threatening to call the police if Tufty did not return home immediately. Giuseppangelo had composed what seemed to him a masterpiece of a letter in which he explained to his father that he could not return because important business detained him in Milan. (*Papa, if only you could see how wonderful it all is. How many opportunities there are!*) Then, silence.

Had Italiano Baroni really decided to let his son have a go at making his fortune in the metropolis? To be on the safe side, Tufty avoided policemen. This silence from his father didn't seem good to him. Probably, one of these days . . .

"Giuseppangelo Baroni, what are you doing here in Milan? I have come to take you back home."

Tufty jumped. A voice really had spoken the words out loud! A dark figure stood motionless in the caretaker's doorway.

"The cops!" cried Tufty, and threw his letter into the air. He leaped to his feet, sending the table flying, and hurled himself toward the window, the only way of escape with the door blocked.

It wasn't dangerous, for the caretaker's room was on the ground floor. But he was caught by the ear even before he reached the window, half open in the pale winter sunshine.

Tufty's eyes were tight shut, partly from pain and partly from fear. He was already picturing himself on the train for Marzamemi, handcuffed like a criminal.

His captor let go, but the hold on his ear had been so firm that he still felt he was a prisoner. He ventured to open one eye—then opened them both very wide.

Standing in front of him, fresh-faced and smiling, was Giuseppangelo Castronuovo, his kindly godfather.

"Oh!" exclaimed Tufty, and his hair stuck straight

up with astonishment. Castronuovo bent down and picked up the letter addressed to him.

" 'Respected godfather,' " he read aloud, making himself a little bow. " 'This letter comes to bring you my respectful greetings and to say that I am in good health and hope you are likewise.'

"Thank you," another little bow, "I'm not too bad.

" 'Finding myself in Milan on business . . .' " Castronuovo looked at Tufty and tried hard not to laugh.

"Ah, so you're in Milan on business? Excellent. I'm here on business myself. Perhaps we can get together, eh?"

Tufty looked at him warily. Could his godfather be teasing him? "Mmmm," he said after a moment's hesitation. "Of course, but I don't think we deal in the same kind of goods."

"Oranges," said Castronuovo tersely.

"Homework," answered Tufty.

"What?" It was his godfather's turn to stare in amazement. Then he burst out laughing. "What do you do? Buy it or sell it?"

"Sell it, naturally. And I don't even need any capital to get started. It's all inside here," Tufty said, tapping his forehead. "But today I lost a hundred lire."

"And how did that happen?"

"Oh well, I earned it, but then I spent rather a lot on the writing paper and the pen and the stamp and so on."

"To write to me?" Castronuovo asked.

Tufty nodded.

"So in fact I owe you a hundred lire?"

Giuseppangelo shrugged as if to say, "It's up to you."

"Right!" his godfather said with a grin. He took a hundred lire from his wallet and handed it to Tufty, who was overjoyed; but he didn't let his feeling show.

"Now then," went on Castronuovo. "Let's hear your reasons for not wanting to go home. From what your father writes to me I gather you have no desire at all to do so."

Tufty tilted his chin, not wanting to go into details. In his heart of hearts he felt a little guilty, but only a little. Our family ties and our longing for adventure often seem to conflict. What can we do? Choose between the two? Independence does not necessarily put an end to family feeling; it can even strengthen it. Tufty did love his home and the place where he was born, but he did not want to leave Milan. He pushed a foot from a white tile to a black one to a green. He couldn't reach the next white one without losing his balance.

"So what you really want is to go to school here in Milan?" asked his godfather, folding the letter and putting it in his pocket.

Tufty nodded emphatically.

Well, why not? Castronuovo mused to himself. It

takes courage to fend for oneself in life. I was left on my own at twelve and I managed to get on. The great thing is to find the work one wants to do and to work at it hard. Giuseppangelo is a good boy and has real aptitude for study. Why shouldn't I help him?

He looked at his young godson. "How about your books?" he asked.

Giuseppangelo smiled. "I brought them with me, along with my guitar."

"And who is this gentleman?" asked Signora Pierina, setting the empty basket down on the kitchen floor.

"He's my godfather," Tufty said proudly. "Giuseppangelo Castronuovo. His name is the same as mine."

"Sit down, sir, make yourself at home. Here is a chair. What can I offer you? I'm afraid this is only a poor household."

Tufty's godfather sat down in the little room without the slightest awkwardness. "You keep it very clean. I've heard very nice things about you, Signora."

The caretaker clasped her hands and blushed. "Well well, so you know of me? This gentleman knows me!"

"Certainly I know of you, and I am delighted to make your acquaintance now in person."

"Have you been talking to Turi, then?"

"Yes indeed. To track down this crazy godson of mine—he's a little odd, isn't he?—I first had to get hold of Turi. He seems to possess a magic flute, this Turi, or rather a magic clarinet," Castronuovo said, smiling.

"Are you Sicilian too, sir?" asked the caretaker.

"Through and through," said Castronuovo.

"I've never managed to get to Sicily," Signora Pierina said. "And to think that my son was killed down there. But that was many years ago. I have never seen his grave."

"I'm so sorry. Where was he killed?"

"Wait a minute. I'll tell you."

She took a key from her apron pocket and opened the top drawer of her desk. She took out a second key and unlocked a trunk standing in the corner of the bedroom. She dug out an old purse and from it she pulled a bundle of papers and handed one of them to Castronuovo. It was the death certificate authorized by the military hospital at Cassibile.

"1944. The war."

There was something so sad about the way Castronuovo spoke and about the look on Signora Pierina's face that Tufty found himself saying, "Wars mean many, many deaths."

"Who told you that?" asked his godfather.

"Antonio. Orestes the hunchback said it to him," Tufty said. "He said it was something to remember. He who kills will be killed."

"I don't know who Orestes the hunchback is," said the surveyor. "But what he says is right, Giuseppangelo. Wars should never be allowed to happen."

"But why do people make wars then?" asked Tufty.

"They think wars will get them somewhere," Castronuovo replied.

The caretaker looked at him. She did not quite understand all this, and kept silent. She put away the papers and the purse, locked the trunk and put away the keys without speaking.

"Well, my dear boy," said Castronuovo, getting up. "I really can see no harm in leaving you in Milan for a few months, providing your business turns out all right. Let us go to a school and I'll ask the headmaster to transfer your enrollment from Syracuse to Milan. Now be a credit to me, and do yourself justice!"

Tufty was so thrilled and excited that he actually had to hold down the unruly red hair which again was sticking straight up all over his head.

"I'll see what I can do to pacify your father," added Castronuovo. "I shall be coming back here often on my own 'business' so I can keep an eye on you."

Tufty wriggled gleefully and winked at Rosalia and Signora Pierina behind his godfather's back as he went out. Then abruptly he pulled himself together and behaved like a perfect model schoolboy.

The following day he enrolled at one of the high schools in Milan, and was at last able to launch his "business" in an organized fashion.

CHAPTER SIX

Antonio's Day Out

Wɪᴛʜ ᴛᴜꜰᴛʏ's ʜᴇʟᴘ, Antonio had written a letter to Orestes, telling him that he had not forgotten him and often thought about him. He had also written to his father, saying that he was doing well in Milan and was sure to make his fortune.

His father had not replied, for the simple reason that he did not know how to write. He had got Don Pietro to read the letter to him, but there was no time to send an answer. The news that Antonio was in the North, in a big industrial city, and about to make his fortune, did not seem to him surprising. In fact it was a dream come true.

Down in Sicily, they were always saying, "Here we starve. If you want to make your fortune, go to work in the North!" It was a sort of legend, and now it was actually happening. Antonio was in Milan. There could be no doubt that he was making, or would soon be making, his fortune.

Just at the moment, however, there was no sign of a fortune, nor indeed of any work at all.

Antonio had knocked on every door, had gone into every shop which sold pottery, to ask if they needed a craftsman. They had looked at him in astonishment, and some had simply burst out laughing.

Up there—on the frozen mountain—it was very different from the market at Noto, where you could soon find out who made the things on sale. Instead, here everything was complicated, impersonal and mechanical. There were only enormous factories, and none of them wanted to take on extra workers. Every job was filled.

Making one's fortune on the great frozen mountain was not nearly so easy as it had seemed in daydreams in Marzamemi.

Antonio could not bear to give up and go back home. For the moment Tufty was helping him out by giving him a share of what he earned from his business. It was terribly cold. After a while Antonio began to feel ashamed of being kept by Turi and he invented a nonexistent job. Besides, Turi often went without a meal so that Giangi and Rags should not go hungry.

One day Antonio and Tufty came upon an old beggarman with an unruly gray beard. He was weighed down by the drum on his back. He played it with his right foot, which was connected to the instrument by a complicated contraption, At the same time he rattled some metal disks above the tambourine with his left foot. An accordion was slung across his stomach. Now and then he would stop under the windows of a house and play a little concert. When he had finished he would cry out: "After all, we've all got to eat!"

And he was quite right. You couldn't argue with him. You have to eat or else you die. It's a law of nature. Yet this law is often broken. Some people have plenty to eat, others have very little, and some have nothing at all.

When Castronuovo departed, he left a little money with Turi to provide for Tufty, and he gave Turi himself a present of a thousand lire—a vast sum.

Antonio had heard that one of the most important pottery factories was on Lake Maggiore, some way out of Milan.

The train went from a little station on the far side of the city. It was dark and smoky, dripping with moisture and gushing clouds of steam.

Tufty had bought the tickets. Sitting face to face on the hard wooden seats, he and Antonio traveled along, silent and serious. They were very much aware of the importance of what they were doing.

Antonio was going because he had to, and of course it wasn't absolutely necessary for Tufty to go along.

But this was just what made the trip fun for him; it was a sort of holiday.

A thick fog, as thick as smoke, hid the countryside. Then all at once little clumps of pine trees began to appear, sometimes blocking out the houses. It was as if the pines were mysteriously sweeping away the fog.

Suddenly a high mountain appeared in the distance, covered with snow. Tufty could hardly believe his eyes; he rubbed them but the mountain was still there. He made Antonio look, too—they could see clearly through the windows now. "How beautiful!" he exclaimed.

At the foot of the mountain lay a mirror of water. Suddenly, for no apparent reason, the boys had the old feeling of sea and sand under their feet.

They stepped out of the train right beside the lake and there were mountains all around. The water was very calm and still, almost motionless.

They walked along the edge of the lake to the dock. They were feeling nervous and ill at ease. This was water, but it was not like the sea. The shore on the other side was edged with little mountains, too; one could almost reach across and touch them. Everything looked unreal and artificial. Even the little white ferryboat which was crossing from the other side looked unreal. It moored alongside the dock and the sailors on board looked different, somehow.

An enormous shining black car began to move forward slowly. It came off the steamer and onto the dock without rocking it at all. The passengers got out, exclaimed loudly in some foreign language and started snapping photographs.

Then a dilapidated old truck, loaded with cheap wares and rolled-up canvas and trestles, made its way noisily onto the boat. Suddenly Tufty left the railing and went to buy a ticket.

"I'm going across!" he announced excitedly to Antonio.

The steamer pulled away, taking Tufty with it.

"There isn't much traffic, because it's winter."

Antonio turned around. A girl with chestnut pigtails was leaning on the parapet, waving to someone on the boat.

"Whom are you waving to?" asked Antonio.

"Papa," the little girl answered proudly. "He's the captain."

"Oh," Antonio looked at her with respect. He had never met a captain's daughter before.

"In summer, it's crowded with cars. They almost fight to get on. There is a waiting line that goes way down there." The girl pointed along the lakeside past the square. She paused, stared at Antonio and asked, "Who are you?"

Antonio was rather at a loss. What could he say? Who was he exactly?

"I'm . . . my name is Antonio." Sometimes the first name is as good as anything.

The girl looked at him again. She was happily walking along the iron railings beside the dock.

"You don't come from around here, do you?" she asked.

Antonio shook his head. "How can you tell?"

"Around here everybody knows everybody else. I know the people on the other side of the lake, too. I often go across with Papa. Besides, you talk funny," she said.

"Funny?" Antonio was rather offended.

She nodded, jumping down from the lowest rail. "How old are you?"

"I'm fourteen today," Antonio said.

"Oh! Happy birthday! I'm twelve. Has your mother made you a cake with candles?"

"My mother is in Marzamemi."

"Where's that?"

"In Sicily."

"Oh!" The little girl stopped climbing about and stared at Antonio with interest and the beginnings of a new respect. "That's a long way away. I learned about it at school, you know. Sicily is like the triangle on the toe of Italy's boot. Italy looks as if it's playing football."

"Yes," murmured Antonio.

"Then you haven't anyone to make you a cake with candles?"

"I haven't told anyone, and anyway I don't know what a cake with candles is."

"You don't know what it is? But . . . it's a cake . . . you don't know what a cake is?" she said, her hazel eyes wide with amazement. "It's a sort of sweet thing, about this big . . ."

"Ah, a cassata!"

"Yes, if you like. And you stick in the same number of candles as your age and light them, and then you have to blow them all out with one puff."

"Only one puff? Why?"

"Because then you'll have everything you wish for in the next year. If you don't, you get nothing."

"So if I had some candles I could blow them all out with one puff and then I'd be able to find some work."

"You are looking for work?"

"Yes."

"Doing what?"

"Pottery is my craft," Antonio said proudly.

"There are lots of factories here in Laveno. One is a great big enormous place. It sends stuff all over the world."

"All over the world?" Antonio almost groaned aloud.

"That's what Papa said," replied the girl, rather taken aback. "There's a system of little trolleys which runs directly from the factory to the freight trains waiting in the station."

Suddenly it all seemed huge and hostile. Great rows of machines kneaded the clay, vast ovens baked it, thousands and thousands of pieces were made at once, no one worried about a broken dish or a misshapen soup bowl. Everything was big, mechanized and impersonal.

"Are you sad?" asked a small voice beside him.

Antonio looked at the captain's daughter and noticed the golden flecks in her eyes. He nodded, swallowing.

"There are smaller factories, too. Much smaller," she said. "If you like, I can come with you." She took Antonio's hand and he let her show him the way.

They all said no. The very last one, a little old man with steel-rimmed spectacles and a black apron, scratched his round bald head and said, "Not right now. But I might well be able to use you in a little while when my assistant leaves to do his national service. Come back again then. O.K.?"

Unfortunately people are more interested in today than tomorrow. It is here and now that counts. Tomorrow they may have grown desperate, or even starved.

It was almost dark when they came back to the dock, and a mist was rising from the lake.

"Thank you, Maria," Antonio said. They were sad.

"What will you do now?" Maria asked.

Antonio shrugged.

In silence they watched the lake grow dark. The ferryboat was drawing near. If he had been alone, Antonio would have cried. He felt the little girl grasp his hand. There was no need to speak.

The boat came alongside. Tufty had red cheeks and bright eyes from standing in the prow facing the wind.

Suddenly Maria said, "I will let you know when Nando leaves for his national service. I know him. Tell me your address."

Antonio told her Number 15 and the street in Milan. Maria repeated it several times. "I'll remember it. Good-bye." She stood on tiptoes and gave Antonio a swift kiss on the cheek. Then she ran off to meet her father, who was just coming out of the captain's cabin.

When they arrived in Milan it was dark and freezing cold. Antonio and Tufty didn't dare look at each other. Antonio still had no job. He was terribly aware that this had been his best, his only chance; and he had lost it. There wouldn't be another one.

They dawdled through the streets, too downhearted to go home. In the square people were crowding around a big stall with lights and a loudspeaker. "Just one turn of this wheel can win you a bicycle, ten bottles of wine, two bottles of liqueur, or a doll, whichever you choose. Fifty lire a try."

A few people tried and won a cheap tie, or a little

fur monkey on a piece of elastic, or nothing at all. Nobody ever seemed to win one of the big prizes.

Tufty looked in his pocket. His last hundred lire. Well, he was having an extravagant day, so why not have a go? Any one would have done the same. In two tries he won nothing.

They set off again.

The street outside Milan's most famous restaurant was crammed with cars. In the lower part of the restaurant window, fish were swimming around in a glass tank, and in the upper part live lobsters were trying vainly to climb up mounds of salad. There were great pyramids of fresh fruit in the corners, and a gorgeous display of truffles and chickens and sweets.

On the opposite side of the street was a more modest establishment with white net curtains screening the windows. Next to the menu and price list, a painted card—with a photograph of the rooms inside—announced that there was dancing to an orchestra every evening on the big covered terrace.

Antonio and Tufty pushed open the door and went inside.

CHAPTER SEVEN

Friends Are Not for Sale

SNOW.

When Giangi and Rags woke one morning, they were aware of a strange, muffled silence in the darkness outside.

They ran to the window. The streetlamps were still lighted, it was dark and snow was falling. White flakes fluttered down past the lamplight into the shadows. Now the ground had two coverings—the asphalt and, on top of that, this new, mysterious white stuff. Snow.

There were a few shovel marks here and there, but they barely showed and another white layer soon settled over them.

Turi sent the two children and Tom over to Signora Pierina with instructions that they were not to go out. With her, at least, they would be warm.

It snowed all day. Giangi and Rags pressed close against the window, they were so fascinated.

The next day the snow had stopped, but the sky was still overcast. In spite of Turi's orders, Giangi, Tom and Rags went out to inspect the snow. They went into the public gardens, which were all fenced in to make sure that no one made off with anything. It was almost as if the railings had, in fact, protected the snow. Unspoilt, it glistened like millions of tiny diamonds.

Now and then the branches of the pine trees would grow tired, and with a heavy thud they would let great lumps of snow slip into the drifts at their feet.

From somewhere in the gardens came the sound of voices; they echoed strangely in the great stillness of the snow. The city was at a standstill. There were no buses or cars running. The distant scraping of shovels was lost in the muffled whiteness.

The two children and the dog followed the voices and came to a little clearing with a large fountain. Children of about their own age were playing there, throwing snowballs at one another.

Giangi, Rags and Tom stopped to watch, in utter astonishment. They had not known that you could play with snow. Rags fingered the pink shell in his pocket. Looking for shells, throwing snowballs—perhaps they had more in common than it might seem: two different games, but both great fun.

They went up to the fountain. Goldfish were swimming around beneath a light film of ice; now and then they would rise toward the surface (expecting to find water, but there was no more water) and bump their heads against the transparent wall of ice.

Nobody asked Giangi and Rags to play. Rich people's children play only with each other.

In a corner, a little apart from the others, stood a small boy of about five; he was frowning and pouting and looking extremely bored.

"Come and play, dear! Come and play!" His English governess, tall and skinny as a rake, was trying vainly to make him stop sulking and join in the snowball fight. She had even ventured to make a snowball herself, and to throw it—very, very gently—at the middle of his fur-trimmed camel-hair coat. The child was furious, stamped his foot and ordered her to brush the flakes off him. "Clean it off at once, you horrid old thing!" The governess brushed him with her woolen glove. "You must speak English, you know."

"Pooh!" was the reply.

But when he noticed the little group leaning shyly against the fountain, the small boy began to show faint signs of interest. He pointed at Tom and said something to the governess.

The woman came over to the children. "Want to play with the dog," she said in very bad Italian.

"You?" asked Rags.

The little boy had come up to them. "He does," the governess said.

"Oh!" they said and looked doubtfully at each other.

The boy stretched out his hand to seize Tom, who bared his teeth and backed away, growling.

"Your dog?" the Englishwoman asked Rags.

"Mine," said Giangi.

The little boy stamped his foot and cried, "I want to play with the dog!"

"Be quiet, dear, be quiet. He is a wicked dog, you see," said the governess soothingly. "It is better not to play with him."

But the boy, growing more and more furious, replied in English, "No, he is not. You are a wicked, a wicked, a wicked."

"Hush, you bad boy! Come along now." She tried to drag him away. That finished it. The boy turned on her like a little wildcat and began hitting at her wherever he could reach her. The more the woman tried to quiet him, the more he lashed out. He nearly sent her glasses flying off her nose.

At this point, Tom, excited by the battle, began to bark furiously and leaped all over them. Rags and Giangi tried vainly to control him.

"Down, Tom, down!" "Tom! Come here, Tom!"

It was no use. There was a moment of complete confusion, and then the governess landed flat in the snow, with Tom bounding around her.

The boy stood quiet for a moment, bewildered, and then he began to laugh and laugh and laugh. The poor woman, sitting in the snow, put on her glasses and straightened her hat with as much dignity as possible, muttering, "You horrid, ill-behaved child."

When he had calmed down a little, the boy approached Giangi. "I like your dog," he said. "Will you sell him to me?" Giangi grasped Tom by the scruff of his neck, hugged him close and shook his own head fiercely in refusal. Rags drew near to back him up.

"Ann," the boy addressed his governess imperiously. "I *will* have this dog. You understand? I will. You must buy him or I'll tell my mother to send you home to England."

The Englishwoman came up to them and, in her dreadful Italian, asked, "You sell dog?"

The two friends burst out laughing. "No, we absolutely no sell dog," answered Rags, imitating her accent.

"Oh!" She was offended and turned back to the little boy. "They no sell. Come along, Guido."

Guido started stamping his feet in the snow again and shrieked, "I want to buy this dog. I want him, I want him!"

Rags and Giangi thought it was wise to move away, keeping a firm hold on Tom.

The child ran after them, pulling his governess

along. "Mama will give you whatever you want. She would even give you a million lire if you asked her, wouldn't she, Ann?"

"Oh really, a million for a *dog*, Guido," she exclaimed indignantly. "Don't be silly."

"I'm not being silly," Guido retorted in English. "I want that dog."

"In that case, I'll ask your mother to buy you a dog tomorrow," she said, trying to pacify him.

"Not tomorrow, today!" he shouted.

"Yes, yes, all right. Today. Now. When your mother comes."

"You don't understand anything, anything at all!" screamed Guido in a burst of hysterical anger. "You horrid old thing! I want *this* dog, see? Not another tomorrow, or even today. This one, this one, this one!"

Giangi, Rags and Tom were fascinated; they stared at the child as if he were an animal in the zoo. He was screaming and yelling and purple in the face. Down one of the paths came a woman in a magnificent fur coat.

"Mama! Mama!" Guido cried, running toward her the moment he saw her.

"What is it, my treasure? What's happened?" asked the woman, suddenly alarmed by the fury in her son's face.

Guido shouted, "I want the dog! I want the dog!"

"I'll buy you one, love. You shall have as many dogs as you want. What happened, Ann?" she asked anxiously.

"Oh, madam!" said Ann, at the end of her endurance. "I ask children, but they no sell dog. Then I say you buy dog tomorrow, today. Guido want only this dog, nothing else." She lapsed into English again. "I'm at my wits' end, madam. What can I do?"

"Why does it have to be this dog?" asked the woman, eying Tom with disgust. "Can't you see how ugly he is? Tomorrow, or even this afternoon, I'll buy you a much nicer one with a shiny coat . . ."

"No, no, no!" Guido began to shriek again. "*You* don't understand anything either. I want this dog, and only this dog!"

"But why?"

"Because he made Ann go head over heels in the snow. He's a funny dog," the child answered.

The fur-coated lady sighed and turned to Giangi and Tom. "Will you sell me your dog? I'll pay you whatever you ask."

"No, madam," replied Rags quickly. "He's an ugly old dog. You'd better not buy him."

"I'm not letting anyone have him, not even for a million," said Giangi.

"Not even for a million! Why not?"

"Because Tom is my friend," replied Giangi.

There was a stunned silence; they were all a bit awed. Here was this child, saying that you do not sell your friends. His words, echoing in that snowy stillness, were somehow very impressive.

Without any warning, the little boy started stamping and screaming all over again.

At last the lady, on a sudden inspiration, said, "Listen, children, why don't you come home with us? Then you won't be leaving your dog. Guido will calm down, and perhaps tomorrow he will be content with another poodle, just like yours. How's that?"

Giangi and Rags looked at each other, embarrassed and uncertain. Guido, who had been listening, quieted down.

"Yes, yes," he said, "that's a good idea! He must come too, he must come too."

"I'll give you a wonderful present, if you'll come," added the lady.

"I'm not selling the dog," Giangi repeated.

"I promise you'll keep the dog," the lady insisted, "and I'll still give you a present if you'll come. Tomorrow you can go home."

Suddenly Rags said, "We never have enough money. You go, and I'll tell Turi to come for you tomorrow." Then, turning to the lady, he said, "I must know your name, and see where you live."

A magnificent car, as big and comfortable as a room,

was waiting outside the gates of the gardens, with chains on its tires to help it through the snow. They all climbed in. The chauffeur started up and in a few minutes they were in front of a beautiful marble house in a quiet, exclusive avenue.

There they parted. Giangi and Tom, still rather reluctant, disappeared through the marble entrance. Ahead of them went the fur-coated lady, the English governess, and the triumphant Guido.

Rags turned and walked off home. It was the first time in many months that he had felt lonely.

It had begun to snow again.

CHAPTER EIGHT

The Boy Wonders

FOR SOME DAYS now the card hanging in the window of the Risorgimento Restaurant had carried a new announcement: GREAT ATTRACTION! THE TWO BOY WONDERS, ANTONIO AND GIUSEPPANGELO, WILL ENTERTAIN YOU WITH FOLK SONGS, ACCOMPANYING THEMSELVES ON THE ACCORDION AND GUITAR.

Boy wonders? Yes, you will have guessed who they were. Our friends Antonio Messina and Giuseppangelo Baroni, otherwise known as Tufty.

Tufty certainly made the most of his abilities. He found his lessons easy? Well then, he would sell homework. He could play the guitar? Well then, he would make people pay to listen to him. It was all so simple!

Antonio was less happy about things. He had accepted the restaurant proprietor's offer, of course, but he did not consider this real work.

To lounge about all day and then go out every evening, and Sunday afternoons too, and strum away on a little platform, while people sat around at small tables eating and drinking—all this seemed humiliating. Antonio's strong arms were for working, not just playing the accordion.

How had all this come about?

Antonio and Tufty hadn't really intended it. They had wandered into the restaurant that evening in a rather dazed state, a result of tiredness and hunger. They had gone right through to the back where, according to the card outside, dancing took place, and had ordered coffee and two slices of cake each. They hadn't a lira between them.

Tiredness, worry, and disappointment had made them so desperate they didn't care what they did.

So they ordered the cake, which was delicious, and the coffee, with its mound of frothy cream.

Tufty could not take his eyes off the orchestra, especially the guitarist.

During an intermission, the musicians came down from their stand, leaving their instruments on their chairs. Tufty leaped onto the platform, seized the guitar and began to play.

At first nobody paid any attention to him. Then a rather nasty waiter tried to chase him off, but the manager signaled him to leave the boy alone, and came closer so that he could hear better. Some of the customers began to notice what was going on and gathered around the stand, greatly amused. Then Tufty burst out singing. The people applauded and cried, "Bravo!" At this point the manager came over. Tufty—nothing could stop him now—pointed out Antonio, who had retreated to a corner, and introduced him as his friend, who would accompany him on the accordion.

They were engaged there and then, at a small, but respectable, salary. And they didn't have to pay for the coffee and cakes.

Turi lived from one crisis to the next. Now and then his boys would disappear and there might be no sign of them for several hours, even for a whole day at a time. Then they would turn up again, as often as not full of some extraordinary adventure. Signora Pierina, too, could never relax. She had taken her eyes off them for only a moment on that terrible snowy day, but it had been time enough for Giangi, Tom and Rags to slip away from Number 15. The time they were gone had seemed to her an eternity.

At last Turi and Rags arrived at her apartment.

Rags recited to her and Rosalia (and Turi, who was hearing it for the umpteenth time) the story of what had happened to Giangi and him that morning.

"What a business!" exclaimed Turi, clutching his head in his hands. "Why do these things always have to happen to you two?"

"Well, well, well!" said the Signora, clasping her hands in despair. Then she replaced her glasses firmly on her nose and went back to ironing shirts.

But, the next day, when it was suggested that Giangi should stay awhile with the Vallis' spoilt little boy, it was she who cheered Turi and persuaded him to accept the offer.

"What's wrong with it, eh, Turi? Giangi is well looked after there. He eats and sleeps in comfort, and at least it gives you a chance to save a bit. You should save a little with all these children to look after. It's dangerous not to have something put aside. You never know what may happen." She was quite right, of course.

Turi went to visit Giangi every day when his music lessons were over, and Giangi, amused by the novelty, was quite happy in Guido's home.

But one evening Rags did not come home. And he wasn't seen the next day either. He had disappeared.

CHAPTER NINE

Rags' Protest

Rags had gone away when he realized that Giangi was staying on at Guido's house.

Jealousy? Perhaps. Rebelliousness? That too. A protest? Surely.

And yet he had encouraged Giangi to go home with Guido. Rags had grown up with hardship; he knew money was important. He knew what suffering came from not having enough of the stuff, and he did not want his small friend, his only real friend, to suffer as he had. He felt very protective toward him, and wanted Giangi to have the lovely present the rich lady had promised.

He had not thought that Giangi would stay long.

Now he was protesting against the fact that anyone could be allowed to take away the only person he,

Rags, aged eight, really cared about; against anyone who could use a real live child as a plaything.

Compared to Guido, Rags had nothing. Nothing. Suddenly his affection for Giangi—of course he had never really told him how he felt—no longer counted for anything. This was the most terrible discovery.

So Rags went out with the firm resolve never to come back. He did not know where he was going, and had no idea of what he was going to do. He was going away in protest, and that was that.

Walking very slowly, his hands in his pockets and his scarf pulled well up over his nose, after a long time he found himself at the station.

All over the city men were scraping and sweeping and carting the snow away. All that beautiful snow! They were throwing it down into dark holes so that nobody could see it anymore. The city was to be covered only by its hard, black, asphalt crust; anything clean and white was not permitted.

If Rags had had any money he *would* perhaps have gone far away. He did not know where, but he would just have jumped onto a train and gone as far away as possible. As it was, he stayed with his nose pressed against the barrier across the entrance to the trains, and watched the people coming and going, laden with suitcases and parcels.

At one point he found himself standing next to a

scruffy-looking boy, scruffier even than himself, which was saying a lot. He stole a quick glance at him. In his hands, all red and swollen with the cold, the boy was holding a small pack of holy pictures.

The stranger was also sneaking a look at Rags.

"What are you doing here?" the boy asked at last.

"What does it matter to you?" demanded Rags sullenly.

"I'm working," the boy said.

"Oh?" said Rags, more interested.

"I'm selling these," the boy went on, waving his pictures. "I make a lot of money."

Rags began to feel hopeful.

"Where did you get them?" he asked after a moment.

"Do you want to work with me?" said the boy. "I'll show you what to do. What's your name?"

"Augusto, but everyone calls me Rags. What's yours?"

"Giovanni. So, are you ready?"

Rags nodded.

"Follow me," said Giovanni.

They stationed themselves at the barrier; porters were coming in and out, laden with luggage. At a swift signal from Giovanni the two boys slipped inside.

They made for the trains; Giovanni was obviously an expert. He looked carefully around, then jumped into the last carriage of a waiting train.

"You must never choose important trains, the through ones or the express. Country trains are much better," whispered Giovanni. Then he suddenly underwent a transformation. He pulled tattered bits of cloth from the sleeves of his threadbare coat, so as to make himself look even more ragged. He rubbed his eyes until they were red, and poked them gently till they filled with tears. Then, dragging his feet in their broken shoes, he set off down the corridor, instructing Rags to follow and watch what he did.

A family was settled in the first compartment. They were surrounded by opened bundles and boxes and were noisily eating bread and cheese.

Giovanni stopped in the doorway and gazed at the food with famished eyes. He stayed so long that finally the mother asked him if he was hungry. Giovanni nodded; a tear trickled down his cheek. He held out his hand and offered them the pictures. A little girl took one. The mother put her hand into her bag and at once Giovanni muttered swiftly, "They cost a hundred lire."

The woman stopped abruptly. "A hundred lire?" she demanded, astonished. "You want a hundred lire for those pictures?"

Giovanni said yes and the mother put her bag away. "In that case I shall not even give you ten," she said sharply. "Go away."

Giovanni snatched the picture out of the little girl's hand and made off.

Rags did not understand what was going on.

Giovanni went up to an old lady, gave her a picture and grudgingly accepted fifty lire. And so it went on. Their takings, though they varied greatly, grew steadily.

Then suddenly Giovanni turned on his heels and

started to run, hissing to Rags, "It's the guard!" They jumped off the train and hid behind a water hydrant. After waiting a minute or two, they went back to work. When they had finished, Giovanni announced triumphantly that they had made 3,400 lire.

"Tomorrow I'll do the hospital," he said. "If you want to work with me, you must come tomorrow, too."

Rags wasn't quite sure.

"What do you do with the money?" he asked. Together they went down the stairs, and at the bottom, hidden in a corner between a newspaper stand and the main entrance, they found a man with hair all slicked down with brilliantine. Giovanni went over to him.

"Who's this?" the man asked, indicating Rags.

"He's a friend. He wants to work, too," Giovanni said.

"Oh. All right. How much have you got?" Giovanni pulled out 2,500 lire and handed it to the man. "Is this all?" he demanded.

"That's all," Giovanni said.

Before he finished speaking, the man's hands were rummaging in his pockets. "I've told you already that sort of thing doesn't work with me," the man said, producing the rest of the money. He gave him two hard blows on the ear.

Rags clenched his teeth. "Why is he taking your money?"

"He's the boss," said Giovanni, his hand to his ear. "He gives me the pictures to sell."

"Oh!" Rags' hopes crumbled.

"Here," the man said sharply to Giovanni, holding out 400 lire. "And you," he added, turning to Rags. "If you want to work with me, you'd better understand that I don't want lies and tricks except for the customers' benefit. See?"

Rags retreated a few paces, then spat on the ground in the direction of the man and shouted, "Rat!" He took to his heels and raced out of the station into the square, where dusk was falling and the lamps were already lit.

CHAPTER TEN

The Little Sicilian Group

W<small>HEN</small> <small>THEY</small> finished playing, Antonio and Tufty would sit down at a table off to one side and rest.

Sometimes the manager, a funny little cricket of a man, would bring them a cool drink. Then he would dash away again to invite some unescorted lady to dance, and would lead her off in complicated steps.

Antonio and Tufty would watch the dancers; they found them very amusing. There was a group of boys with long heavily brilliantined hair, gold chains on their wrists and striped suits, who sat in a group and went around asking all the girls to dance.

This particular group was often seen there and they were great admirers of Antonio and Tufty, who took turns entertaining the audience. The group would invite them over to their table, or one or another of them would wander across to talk to Antonio.

196

As for Tufty, he was full of bright ideas. One Sunday afternoon he dragged Rosalia and her tambourine to the Risorgimento Restaurant. This was a great success. Much encouraged, Tufty planned to get Giangi to come along with his marranzanu the following Sunday, and Tom too.

The only one missing was Rags.

All their efforts to trace Rags had been in vain. Turi was convinced that if he went to the police looking for a missing child he would be arrested. No one would believe that the children had followed him of their own free will. So he made inquiries himself, with the help of Antonio and Tufty. Turi had not had the courage to say anything to Giangi. On Sunday when he went to get him at Guido's house, to take him to the Risorgimento Restaurant, he said nothing about Rags. In answer to Giangi's insistent questions, he said that Signora Pierina had sent him on an errand.

The four children were a great success. Rosalia sang, Tufty sang too; then they sang a duet. But when Tom did a dance on his hind legs, accompanied by Giangi on the marranzanu, they nearly brought the house down. Tom was doing an encore, accompanied by the whole group, when who should appear in the doorway but Giuseppangelo Castronuovo. He stared in amazement for a minute; then he smiled and sat down at a table. Giuseppangelo Baroni, known as

Tufty, spotted him, allowed himself a stealthy wink, and then as soon as the piece was over hurtled across to say hello.

"Well?" demanded Castronuovo.

"Well, here I am. I've organized the Little Sicilian Group," said Tufty, very pleased with himself.

"The Little Sicilian Group advertised on the poster outside?" asked his godfather.

"That's us!" said Tufty triumphantly. "They pay us to play," he added, to make things quite clear.

The surveyor laughed, much amused. "And how's school?" he asked.

"Excellent, excellent," said Turi, coming over to join them. "He's not quite such a cuckoo as you might think."

"And so now we're going on the stage, eh?" added Castronuovo. "In fact this godson of mine is full of bright ideas."

He looked hard at Tufty. His hair was standing on end, his eyes were sparkling and he was grinning happily; his fingers were inkstained as usual. Castronuovo had a sudden flash of hope. For an instant, amidst the confusion of the dancing couples, the music, the steaming tea, he saw someone to whom he could pass on his ideas. His cherished plans for improving conditions for the people in the South had been thwarted so often; perhaps Tufty would be able to make them come true.

"Who knows?" murmured Castronuovo.

He shook himself, looked around him, smiled at Tufty, who was gazing at him ecstatically. He asked Turi how his music was going and whether he had any plans.

Turi became animated. He had not been doing at all badly so far; he had passed the examinations to qualify for the advanced course.

They talked about Rags' disappearance, too, and Signor Castronuovo promised to do whatever he could to help.

Giangi had asked for Rags several times. Turi had always managed to put him off. He was almost relieved when the time came to take Giangi back to Guido's house.

Giangi and Tom found the Valli house in an uproar. Giangi made his way cautiously along the hallway and met the doctor coming out of Guido's room with Signora Valli. "He has calmed down now, Signora. You can stop worrying," the doctor was saying.

"If only Giangi and that blessed dog would come back. Ah! Thank heavens, here they are. Giangi, come and see Guido at once. He has cried all day without you," the Signora said, leading him by the hand into her son's room.

Giangi and Tom went inside. There was a cry of joy, a bark from Tom, and then the sound of the children playing.

Signora Valli showed the doctor out herself, though the maid was waiting in the hall.

"Doctor, do you think there is something the matter with Guido?" she asked anxiously.

"Yes, I do," answered the doctor.

"Oh, my God!" she cried. "But what?"

"Sheer boredom," the doctor said.

"Boredom? But we give him everything he wants, everything. Toys, the theater, movies, games. At Christmas he had a miniature electric car, complete with radio and aerial. He and Sardi's son are the only children in all Italy who have one, and it cost a fortune. And now this Sicilian child and the dog . . ."

"Exactly, Signora, exactly," said the doctor. "And I fear the condition may get worse as he grows older."

He went away, leaving Signora Valli very puzzled.

And when Rosalia got back, she found Signora Pierina too was crying, but very quietly. She was sitting in the kitchen, in the dark; now and then she wiped her eyes on the corner of her apron.

Rosalia ran to her, frightened, but the caretaker's crying was calm, almost relieved. Rosalia didn't ask what the matter was; she waited quietly in the darkness.

"My son is coming," said Signora Pierina at last.

Rosalia knew her son was dead. How could he come back? She kept quiet and waited.

"Signor Castronuovo is having him brought back from Sicily. Now I shall be able to visit his grave and put flowers there," said the caretaker.

So on that same Sunday that Guido had cried, Signora Pierina had cried, too. People cry for very different reasons.

CHAPTER ELEVEN

Express Delivery

"I DON'T LIKE that crowd," Tufty said firmly to Antonio one evening. He was referring to the boys with long hair and striped suits who had made friends with Antonio at the dance floor. Antonio shrugged his shoulders. When they reached home, instead of going in with Tufty, he made some excuse and went off on his own. Tufty gazed after him, shaking his head; what was happening made him very uneasy. He closed the door angrily and started to climb the stairs.

Antonio came in very late, tired and heavy-eyed. Next day he disappeared again.

That evening, between one piece of music and the next, Tufty, who was keeping his ears open, overheard a stray remark: "Our plan is just about ready now. Antonio is with us, but since he's new, he'd better just act as lookout. . . ."

The speaker was one of the gang Tufty disliked. He was sitting at a table covered with drinks in the dance room of the Risorgimento Restaurant. Tufty disliked what he had heard even more than he disliked the speaker. He tried to hear more, but when he drew closer, the others lowered their voices. Antonio was among them; he did not even dare look Tufty in the face.

They weren't friends anymore, Antonio and Tufty; that had been clear for some time.

"Is it worth the risk?" asked another boy in the group. Tufty caught the answer, too: "Yes, of course it is. There'll be enough for all of us." They didn't say any more and scattered to find girls and dance. They were up to no good, certainly. Tufty knew for a fact that Antonio was feeling guilty. Otherwise he would surely have told him what was going on.

Tufty was badly worried. What was Antonio up to with that gang? What were they going to do, and when?

Tufty made a private vow that he would keep his eyes and ears open all the time, and that when the moment came he would, if necessary, even use force.

The day came, inevitably, when the plan was ready. Antonio had been getting paler and paler, and had become all shut in on himself. Tufty trailed him everywhere. Finally Antonio even threatened to hit him if he would not go away.

"Everything's ready," announced the leader of the boys one day. Antonio was among them; he turned even paler, if that was possible, and hung his head.

Tufty was some distance away and had not been able to hear what was said, but he saw Antonio's face change and guessed the moment had come.

The group put their heads together in a tight little bunch and had a quick, excited consultation. Tufty could catch only the final instructions: "Tomorrow at the usual place for last arrangements, and tomorrow evening for the job."

Antonio and Tufty went back to the stage to play. Tufty studied his companion through a haze of tears. Tomorrow. Tomorrow evening. The same refrain rang in both their heads, but in very different ways.

Is there no way out? thought Antonio. They are forcing me into it.

What can I do? What can I do? Tufty groaned to himself. It's all because he couldn't find a job. It's all right for me, I don't have to work. But it's different for him. He's a man.

Suddenly Rosalia appeared at the edge of the dance floor. She had something in her hand. She made her way among the tables until she reached the platform. Triumphantly she showed Antonio what she was carrying—a letter for him.

Tufty felt as though a great weight had been taken

from his shoulders. He looked at Rosalia as if she were some kind of miracle. He had no idea what the letter could be about; but if Rosalia had left the house at this hour just to bring a letter, it could only contain good news.

Antonio turned the letter over and over in his hands. At last he decided to open it. He read it slowly, mouthing the words like a child. Tufty watched his expression anxiously, running his inky fingers through his hair.

As he read, Antonio's face seemed to clear and he looked just as he used to. He became a boy again, instead of a man with a hard face and set eyes.

Then his face darkened. He shrugged his shoulders contemptuously and thrust the letter into his pocket.

Tufty's heart sank. Nothing could be done; Antonio was lost.

CHAPTER TWELVE

At the Circus

Guido had not yet tired of Giangi and Tom. Perhaps this was only because he was still afraid of losing them.

And on Sunday afternoons, he was permitted to go with Giangi to the Risorgimento Restaurant. Never in all his life had he spent such wonderful Sundays.

"There's a circus, I want to go to the circus to-morrow."

Instantly Giuseppe the footman was sent out to buy front-row tickets for Guido, Giangi, Ann and Tom. Yes, Tom had a seat to himself, without even a reduced price, because although he wasn't a grown-up, he wasn't a child either.

"What is the circus?" asked Giangi, full of curiosity.

"It's a big tent, with lots of wild animals, and the

tamer, and then there are horses that dance and clowns that make you laugh," explained Guido. "You'll see, it's great fun."

Giangi was very excited. He had never seen anything like that before. That night he dreamed he was in a strange place which could have been the dance floor at the Risorgimento Restaurant, except that it was much larger. An enormous Tom, as big as a horse or even bigger, was dancing to the flute, played by Ann. Giangi, Guido and Rags were sitting together and applauding. Giangi was having a wonderful time, when suddenly he noticed that Rags wasn't beside him anymore. Perhaps he had been missing for some time —and then suddenly, in the dream, a great wave of sadness came over Giangi. But Guido kept laughing and laughing at Tom's antics and all at once Giangi felt very angry. Then he felt sure that if Rags had gone away it was Guido's fault.

Giangi woke with his eyes full of tears, and began to call for Turi. He wanted to go back to him, no matter what. He suddenly wanted very much to escape from this house where he was cared for too well and where there was no Turi and no Rags. The Vallis could quiet him only by reminding him of the circus.

The circus was indeed in an enormous tent. It was stretched over a ring covered with sawdust, and there were seats all around it for the audience.

Suddenly the ring was flooded with bright light; the audience remained in darkness. A voice announced: "Ladies and gentlemen! Welcome to our circus. We now present the famous Hans Franz and his twelve white horses! Hans Franz!" Noisy music burst forth. On the far side of the ring, where there was a large square entrance, the curtains parted and out came a young, fair-haired man. He swaggered along, looking very pleased with himself, a long whip in his hand and his coat covered with gold braid.

The children applauded, and then out came twelve white horses, their manes combed smooth and their bridles gilded. Hans Franz, the man with all the braid, cracked his whip and the horses began to trot around the ring, in line, in time to the music. The horses made all sorts of patterns, and bowed their heads, and stood up on their hind legs; they were amazing.

Next came the Chicago Family. They juggled with balls and clubs all over the ring. Then they climbed up into a sort of human pyramid, the father at the bottom and the children at the top. "Oop-la!" they called out and all of them jumped down and not one broke a leg. Everyone clapped madly.

A girl dressed in pink rode in on the neck of an elephant. Behind her followed six more elephants. A man in silk pantaloons and a turban demonstrated how obedient they were, those huge animals. They too kept time to the music, walking around one behind another, each holding another's tail with his trunk.

Men all in white flew high in the air, right up under the top of the tent, on shining trapezes. They seemed as light as feathers, but they were real men all right.

Giangi watched in amazement. He was more than just pleased, he was ecstatic. The lights, the colors, the golden dust hanging in the air, the strange smell, all the other children clapping and laughing. He could hardly believe it was real.

A comical tune announced the arrival of the clowns. Guido began to laugh excitedly and clap his hands . . . just as in Giangi's dream.

There were five clowns. The first, tall and thin, had huge, fantastic shoes. A tiny clown was sitting on one of the toes, playing a mouth organ. Two others were wearing checked trousers several sizes too large for them and white hats like chefs. The fifth was squeezed into a doll's carriage pretending to be a baby.

They began a pantomime, hitting each other, tripping each other up. They fell down, rolled about and played all kinds of funny tricks. At the end, the four big ones made a circle around the little one, clapping their hands as he played on his mouth organ.

Tom had behaved beautifully until the clowns came in. But from that moment on he began to wriggle restlessly and Ann had to grab him and hold him on her lap to keep him quiet.

But when the clowns, amid tumultuous applause, made one last circle around the ring and passed right by the front row, Tom gave a great yelp, struggled out of Ann's arms, and hurled himself onto the small clown with the mouth organ. The clown was almost knocked over with surprise, but then he began hugging Tom and kissing him. They were clearly on very familiar terms.

There was a moment's pause, then . . .

"It's Rags!" yelled Giangi. Before Ann could stop him he was over the railing and into the arms of the little clown. The two friends hugged each other tearfully while Tom, crazy with excitement, danced around them. The other clowns stared in amazement.

The audience was a little puzzled at first. Then it broke into applause as the clowns, realizing that they were well past the time limit for their act, lifted the two children onto their shoulders and carried them triumphantly out of the ring.

Ann and Guido, too, were astonished at first. Then they ran around to the back where several of the performers had gathered around Giangi, Rags, and Tom to find out just what had happened.

Rags was very proud indeed of his job and his new friends. The oldest clown had found him that hateful evening, wandering through the streets shivering with cold and hunger, and had taken him back to the caravan.

Rags dragged Giangi off to see it.

"This house moves," he said, his eyes shining under his heavy makeup.

"When?" asked Giangi, fascinated.

"When we go to do the show in another town. It moves along in line with all the others."

"Are you going too?" Giangi asked anxiously.

"I don't know," Rags said uncertainly.

"Let's go back together and live with Turi," said Giangi, and hugged him.

"Yes," said Rags, still hesitant. Did he really want to stay with the circus?

"Don't you want to?" asked Giangi.

"I work here," Rags explained. "When I eat, I've earned my food, do you see? And at night, in bed, I know that at last I'm free, I'm free."

Freedom. Freedom. What a wonderful thing. Giangi resolved never to go back to Guido's house.

CHAPTER THIRTEEN

Antonio Keeps an Appointment

As the train traveled along, the high snow-covered mountain suddenly appeared on the horizon. It was the palest rose pink, and looked almost transparent.

The lake was calm and friendly. Antonio found Maria waiting for him by the dock. He had hardly caught sight of her, standing there with her gold-flecked chestnut hair knotted back and falling loose over her shoulders, when he started to feel better. He was like a new person.

He stood and looked at her; they didn't even shake hands.

"Hello," said Maria.

"Hello," Antonio said softly and gave a very faint smile, the first for many weeks. It was so slight that Maria did not even notice it.

"Well, are you pleased?" she asked.

Antonio nodded. "Thank you," he said, taking a deep breath. He was watching the sunlight creeping along the shores of the lake and chasing away the shadows. They huddled below the mountain, moved up over the houses and fled away.

"I never forget things," said Maria. "Papa says so, too."

"Thank you," repeated Antonio, looking at her.

They started walking.

"Nando is leaving in a few days. I wrote to you at once, so you wouldn't miss the chance." The road wound upward toward the little workshop. Maria suddenly stopped, turned to him, and announced, "Today you're coming to lunch with us. Papa wants to meet you and Mama is making a cake, a—"

"A cassata," interrupted Antonio.

"A cassata," Maria nodded laughing.

"But of course it's not exactly the same. Cake has almond icing," added Antonio.

They walked on in silence.

"Is cassata nice? I've never eaten it."

"Lovely. I've really had it only once, in Syracuse," Antonio said. "I remember it tasted of flowers."

They arrived at the workshop of the little old man with the black apron. He received Antonio kindly and, after quickly trying him out, took him on at once in place of Nando.

"This good little girl here," old Anselmo said to Antonio, "has kept coming around to find out when Nando was leaving. What a little schemer! She wanted the job for her own 'discovery,' didn't you, Maria?"

Maria smiled.

Maria's father, the captain, had a small house with a garden and a part of the lake all to itself. The cake which Maria's mother had made was delicious, and the narrow strip of sand at the edge of the lake was almost as good as the seashore for walking barefoot. Maria and her mother thought this an extraordinary thing to do. The captain laughed—but then men understand each other better.

Tufty was already in bed when Antonio returned, but he wasn't asleep. He sat up in bed, his hair all on end with anger and misery.

"Where have you been?" he demanded curtly.

Antonio took a little pink card from his pocket and threw it on the bed. "That's where I've been."

Tufty turned the card over and over between his fingers. Milan–Laveno return ticket. Thank heavens! He lay back with a sigh of relief. Even his hair seemed to settle down normally on his head. He kissed the ticket and flicked it away. Then something occurred to him.

"You did get it?" he asked.

"Yes, I've got it." Antonio said without looking at him. "For the time being."

"Oh," said Tufty slightly disappointed.

"I gave up a sure thing—a great deal of money—for a temporary job," Antonio said, turning away to hide his grin.

Happiness was welling up inside him, yet he couldn't resist tormenting Tufty. Tufty was very fond of him, he knew that. And he too was fond of— A pillow flew at his head. Antonio picked it up and hurled it back at Tufty. A glorious battle followed. They laughed and laughed until tears ran down their cheeks, and at the end the tears were almost real. But they were happy because they were friends again.

CHAPTER FOURTEEN

Turi and Signor Valli Both Have Their Troubles

THE FEW PEOPLE left in the advanced section of the bandmasters' course made anxious inquiries about jobs. In reply they received only vague warnings not to hope for too much. Only a few jobs were available and there would certainly not be enough to go around.

Turi put his head in his hands and thought he would go out of his mind. Why? Why then had he gone through such terrors, worked so hard? Why had he left everything, abandoned it all, sold his pots, pans, mattress, everything he possessed? What was the point of it all? It simply didn't make sense.

How can I go back home? he asked himself. He was penniless; there was nothing inside those four walls he had left in Marzamemi; he had no job.

At about the same time, Signor Valli, Guido's father, was also clutching his head and thinking he would go out of his mind. We all have our troubles.

What was troubling Signor Valli? With a house like his (not counting the one on the sea and the one in the mountains), a cook, a maid, footmen, a butler, an English governess for his son, two drivers for whichever car he felt like using, and an enormous bank account (not to mention his various lands and the farms and buildings all over his property)—what on earth could possibly upset Signor Valli?

The trouble was that when he had tired of the football team he owned, Signor Valli had bought a complete revue company: scenery, costumes, dancers, singers and comedians, the whole outfit.

From that moment, he had not a moment's peace.

The dancers broke their legs; the singers lost their voices; the comedian dropped everything to follow the girl he loved abroad; the director had an attack of depression and had to be invited to breakfast, lunch and dinner every day, along with a couple of faithful friends, to cheer him up.

Every day—no, every hour, every minute—some new disaster occurred.

The latest was the desertion of the company by one of the leading acts, the Double Z Group.

"Don't talk to me. Don't say a single word. Just leave me alone," said Signor Valli one day, sitting down heavily at the table.

"Remigio," said Signora Valli nervously, "Why don't you sell the company, if it causes you so much trouble?"

"AAH!" Signor Valli roared in desperation. "Can't you understand that nobody wants it? That I'm the one and only idiot who could have such a burden foisted on me? That I'm the only man fool enough to pay through the nose for the privilege? Through the nose!" The wretched man groaned aloud and settled down to his chicken with new potatoes and peas.

No one dared to breathe throughout the chicken, potatoes, peas, cheese and fruit, and some tiny chocolate eclairs which melted in the mouth and which even poor Signor Valli managed to enjoy.

While they were sipping their coffee Guido suddenly spoke. "Papa!"

Signor Valli jumped. "What is it, Guido?" He was always strangely indulgent with his son.

"I have a marvelous act for your show."

Signor Valli almost choked on his boiling-hot coffee. "What? What?" he spluttered, and his wife, watching anxiously, caught a flicker of a smile on his face.

"Yes," Guido went on, quite unmoved. "If you'll come with me on Sunday afternoon, I'll show you. And you must buy them for your revue, and pay them a lot of money."

"What do you think I am, my boy?" his father asked. "A machine for making money? Just you get that idea right out of your head, understand?"

"No, that's just what you are, a money machine. And you must buy the orchestra because I say so," retorted Guido, getting excited. "You must come with me to see them on Sunday afternoon."

"Now look here, Guido," Signor Valli began, but his wife interrupted him.

"Please, dear, do go and make him happy. Just this once."

"This once?" exclaimed her husband. "Just this once? Why, I've just about given him the moon! What more do you want?"

"I don't want the moon, I don't want it," Guido began, his voice rising. "I want Papa to buy my friends for his show."

"Aha! Because they're your friends?" interrupted his father. "So they are children?"

"There's Giangi and Tom and the others. Papa, do come and buy the Sicilian Group!"

"Imagine putting children in place of the Double Z Group. Guido, please be quiet and let's hear no more of this," Signor Valli said, lighting a cigarette.

Guido resorted to tears. He screamed and stamped his feet.

"Now, Remigio, do what he wants!" said Signora Valli, trying to calm her son. "Do at least say you'll go with him on Sunday. Then of course you must do as you think best."

"But I'm busy on Sunday! There's a full rehearsal of the revue on Sunday! I can't possibly miss it . . . we're in enough trouble as it is," Signor Valli tried to protest.

By this time Guido was almost having a fit. Ann was sent to call the doctor. Signora Valli knelt by her son in tears and accused her husband: "Look what you've done!"

Signor Valli, greatly distressed, was forced to give in and promise that he would go with Guido that Sunday afternoon.

The minute Guido heard his father give in, he calmed down.

Having made the promise, Signor Valli at once regretted it. He went off feeling he was a defeated man.

Meanwhile, Turi had received a definite answer.

There were only two posts as bandmaster with a salary for life, and Turi's name was not chosen for either of them. Yet everyone said that he was the best in the school. Why had he not been chosen? Turi didn't understand—and it made him very sad.

One of the winners was a nephew of the mayor of the little town where he was to be the new bandmaster. No one really knew why he had bothered to enter the competition at all, since the award had quite clearly been promised to him in advance. As for the other winner, he had powerful connections who had made sure he was given the other position, in his home town. Turi had only his talent, and a large and useless sheet of paper covered with the signatures of distinguished experts.

He was alone, on top of the great frozen mountain, with five children and a dog who trusted him and thought he could do anything. Alone, with no money and no resources.

Alone, and he could not understand why.

CHAPTER FIFTEEN

"Discovered"

Signor valli ordered the rehearsal for the revue to be postponed until the evening, and made arrangements to meet his colleagues at the Risorgimento Restaurant on Sunday afternoon.

When the proprietor saw Signor Remigio Valli, one of the richest and most powerful men in the city, he was overjoyed. He hopped around bowing and scraping, pushing tables together, pulling up chairs, scattering smiles and table napkins, and generally getting the place into a turmoil. Finally he took Signor Valli's order—tea and cakes, just like anyone else. The other gentlemen in his party preferred rolls filled with ham or cold roast meat and beer. They managed to put away an incredible amount.

Once they had settled down, Signor Valli, the producer, the manager, the director, the set designer, the authors of the revue, and several other odd helpers brought out a pile of papers and started arguing.

Guido tried unsuccessfully to attract his father's attention, calling to him and tugging at his sleeve. But Signor Valli would just answer vaguely, "Yes, yes, all right," gaze vacantly at the little platform where the band was without really seeing anything, and then plunge back into the discussion.

Then the producer happened to look up absent-mindedly for a moment, and glanced quite unintentionally at the Little Sicilian Group, who at that moment were in the middle of their performance. He watched for a moment or two, without taking anything in, then suddenly he started really to pay attention. When Tom began to dance, the producer laughed out loud, enjoying himself tremendously. When the others spoke to him he didn't answer, and gradually they too began to watch the little group. They clapped loudly, demanded encores, and generally made a great uproar.

But when the producer turned suddenly to Signor Valli and announced positively, "These children are a real find. I think we should engage them," they were all astounded.

"What do you mean? Engage them?" demanded Remigio Valli nervously. "You're not serious, I hope?"

"I'm perfectly well aware of what I'm saying, and I know my job, my dear Valli," the producer said. There was a heated argument. Eventually one of the authors, too, began to support the idea of signing on the Little Sicilian Group, mostly because he did not want to appear less clever than the producer.

Signor Valli was torn both ways. He was not sure that it was a good idea; on the other hand he had to trust his colleagues' judgment, for they had often proved they knew more about certain things than he did and it was better to leave such things to them.

"Very well," he said at last. "Give them a contract."

Guido, who had stood tense beside his father's chair throughout the discussion, gave a whoop of delight.

Turi was summoned from the corner where he was sitting rather sadly by himself, and told the good news. Naturally he was to be engaged also.

What should he do? Accept, of course.

Turi had never in all his life earned, or even laid eyes on, as much money as he was being offered now.

How could he possibly refuse?

Yet it was certainly not the job he had dreamed of getting after all his trials and disappointments and hard work. He felt capable of taking on the leadership of any band in the world. Instead, here he was once more, as in the old days at Marzamemi, conducting a children's band. But this time it would be his life's work. Or would it?

Part
Three

CHAPTER ONE

Applause

"Oh, what treasures!" gushed the leading lady of Signor Valli's company. Antonio, Rosalia, Rags, Giangi, and Tom were huddled timidly together in a little group at the corner of the stage. "Would you like some candy, darlings?"

"Fifi, Fifi! Come here, Fifi!" The leading lady's dog, a miniature white poodle, had sidled close to Tom and was cautiously sniffing him. She was a very pretty little dog, with a blue collar studded with gold and her hair soft and tightly curled.

Tom recognized her at once. With a shudder he remembered where he had seen her—at the dogs' beauty parlor. Guido had insisted Tom be sent. "Tom must go to the barber so that he can have a really glossy coat, mustn't he, Mama?" Guido had told his mother. Tom had snarled, bared his teeth and dug his claws in. But go he did, and to the most exclusive dog's beauty parlor in Milan.

They had plunged him into a foam bath. It got into his eyes, his ears and his nose, and made him sneeze and spit frantically. All at once he had remembered the taste of the sea at Marzamemi. How good it had seemed. To think that he had never wanted to go into it. He thought sadly of the sun which used to dry him with its soft, gentle fingers and of the seaweed, that great cushion of dry seaweed, on which he had been free to roll. Then, in the tiny shop, stinking with perfumes and antiseptics and disinfectants, he had been put on a special table to be dried. They had used a strange machine which blew out hot air. He hated it.

Then they had clipped him. His beautiful curly hair had been shaved off in great strips, and he had had to stand there, thin and shorn in front of everyone. He had never been so humiliated in all his life. But he had had to put up with it. He had tried to bark and growl, and even to run away. It had done no good; the people in that place were fiends.

At last all he had left were elegant little fur pants and a coy little tuft on his head, exactly like the stuffed dog from the Grand Store.

And he had felt cold, too. Then—the final indignity

—they had slipped a fine woolen plaid coat, trimmed with leather, on his back and fastened a scarlet, gold-studded collar around his neck.

He had been put in a tiny waiting room until someone came to fetch him. That was where he had seen Fifi wearing the same blue collar, studded with gold.

"Fifi! Fifi!" The sharp tone of the leading lady's voice brought Tom up with a start. Fifi was being summoned. She had to go.

Then came the rehearsal. There were shouts and roars from the producer, despairing sighs from Signor Valli, and loud crashes as pieces of scenery came hurtling down onto the performers. To cap it all, the leading lady, Dora Carrell, chose this moment to have hysterics.

In all this confusion, the Little Sicilian Group's performance was scarcely noticed.

The next night—the evening of the opening—the children received such a burst of applause at the end of their third act (after Rosalia, in a dress all the colors of the rainbow, had sung and danced with her tambourine, Tufty had sung, and Tom had danced to the marranzanu) that they stood for a moment in astonishment.

The footlights held them on a warm, golden island, and they looked out across a vast, dark sea of unknown faces. The audience hung on their every word, their

every gesture. Once the little group had it in their power they could do anything they liked with it. But the audience was equally powerful. Simply by clapping or not clapping, they could either turn the children into stars overnight, or condemn them to dismal failure.

The applause was overwhelming. Turi and the children were swept off their feet; the great waves of clapping thundered in their ears.

The audience clapped on and on. Turi was stunned. He didn't know what to do next. He looked around and in the wings he saw the producer, the authors, the manager, and Signor Valli triumphantly signaling him to go on playing.

Turi signaled to the children, and they played an encore—"Beautiful Sicily." Turi had tears in his eyes.

CHAPTER TWO

Success

THEY SPENT the next day reading the reviews of the opening night. They had been a terrific success.

Signor Valli, lying stretched out in bed, was becoming more and more convinced that he was not only one of the richest and most powerful men in the city, but also one of the cleverest.

Wasn't it he who had bought the revue company in the first place? Wasn't it he who had signed on the Little Sicilian Group in place of the Double Z Group?

"The members of the Little Sicilian Group—the star act of the show—" said the leading city newspaper, "are between five and fourteen years old, and their teacher is a young Sicilian as apparently unspoiled as his pupils. Their performance is one of the most charming and original imaginable. To come across a fragment of that sun-drenched isle and its happy people on our dusty, northern stage is little short of a miracle."

"Does anyone recall that small news item which passed almost unnoticed a few months ago," said another paper, "about the foiling of an armed raid on the Grand Department Store? The heroes were two little Sicilian boys, one aged five and the other eight, and their dog. To our great amazement and delight, we found them again last night—still with their faithful poodle—on the stage of the Old Theatre, where they are playing in the Little Sicilian Group, made up entirely of Sicilian children. They are conducted by a young man who seems to have the heart of a child, too. This little group is one of the most refreshing and delightful acts in the whole show."

They were off!

Every detail of that famous night at the Grand Store had to be dug up and gone over again and again. Giangi, Rags and Tom were photographed and appeared in color on the front of all the big national magazines.

The Grand Department Store presented the two "courageous Sicilian boys" with a refrigerator and the latest model gas stove when they posed for a photograph to be used as an advertisement. And each of them received a marvelous toy car and a complete cowboy outfit.

Presents, invitations to lunches, dinners, official functions and ceremonies—and photographs, endless photographs.

And money.

Turi and the children could now be considered almost rich; they all had new clothes. They gave the stove and the refrigerator to Signora Pierina, their one real friend. And they also presented some big signed photographs to the owner of the Risorgimento Restaurant.

Giangi and Rags were getting tired of all this fuss and excitement. Now, after the success of the first night, they had to appear twice, instead of once, during the performance. In between, they had to wait in the dressing room, their faces plastered with grease paint, almost too tired to stay awake.

"Do you like playing with the little car?" Giangi asked Rags one night.

"Yes," he said, "but the one Amedeo the clown has is much more fun."

"Why?"

"Because he's so tall and has to squash himself up to get inside it."

After a pause, Giangi said, "Why doesn't the pretty lady give us candies anymore?"

"She's not pretty," declared Rags.

"She isn't pretty because she doesn't give us caramels?" Giangi asked.

"No. She's just not pretty, that's all. She's got pretend eyes, all painted. What's more, she kicked Tom."

"Kicked Tom?" Giangi echoed in astonishment.

Rags nodded. "*And* she slapped Rosalia."

"Oh!" Giangi was horrified.

Rags nodded again fiercely. "The other evening, in the part where she goes over to Rosalia and pretends to give her an affectionate pat, she hit her instead." Giangi stared at his friend in amazement. "And she doesn't want to act with us any more," added Rags. "I heard her saying to Guido's father that she doesn't want to play second fiddle to anyone."

The two children gazed at each other. "What *does* she mean?" asked Giangi.

"I've no idea," replied Rags.

They were silent, drowsy from the strong lights around the dressing room mirror.

Rags took his pink shell from his trouser pocket and played with it. It was as light and soft as foam.

"I want to swim," he said at last.

"In the sea," added Giangi.

CHAPTER THREE

The Ogre's Den

ONE DAY THEY were taken to visit an ogre's den. It was a vast room full of bright lights and animals with four noses. At the end of each nose was an eye; all the eyes stared straight at poor Giangi, who started to cry. He felt sure the animals were going to eat him. But they had no mouths, let alone teeth.

He had to be shown that these metal animals were harmless; that they couldn't even move without being pushed by a man in overalls and at the command of other men in white who sat astride them.

"What is it?" asked Giangi, pointing to one of the monsters, now he was sure there was no danger.

"It's a television camera," they told him.

"And that one over there, too?" asked Rags.

"Yes," said the man in white. "They're all television

236

cameras. Each one has a number to distinguish it from the others. Camera one, camera two, camera three. Mine is number two, the most important one. Do you see?"

"Is yours good?" asked Giangi.

"Well, not always," said the man on the camera. "It depends on the director."

"How do you mean?" asked Rags.

The man laughed. "He's that man over there, do you see him? The one who's rushing around so busily. He gives orders, from the director's control room, for the movements we have to carry out."

Another man in a white shirt appeared, with a funny sort of thing on his ear. He said it was time to begin.

"What's that thing on your ear?" asked Giangi.

"With it I can hear the director's orders and give the sign for the show to start."

The cameramen, too, had funny things on their ears, connected to the director's room.

The cameras were very clever. Each of their noses, some longer, some shorter, had a round eye. The whole thing, nose and eye together, was called a lens. Depending on which lens was used, the camera could show people and things close up or far away.

When the cameras began to stare at them, Giangi and Rags could be seen in Syracuse, and Tufty by his godfather in Palermo. But all the time they were really up there on top of the frozen mountain in northern Italy.

What an extraordinary thing!

So extraordinary, in fact, that Orestes the hunchback, who was sitting in a café in Syracuse watching television, felt very strange when he saw his friends there on the screen, playing away while Tom danced, as if it were all perfectly natural. He had to be helped outside to get some fresh air.

Outside, in the cool sea breeze, Orestes wept with emotion. He was overcome by the surprise, and repeated again and again, without really knowing what he was saying, "They were just like them! They were just like them!"

CHAPTER FOUR

All Work and No Play

"Why is playing such hard work?" Giangi asked
Rags one day. They were perched on some packing
cases in the far corner of a movie studio, waiting for
the director to summon them.

"Are we playing now?" Rags asked doubtfully.

"I think so," Giangi said.

"Yesterday they told us to go and play on that beach
over there, where the girl with the long hair is walking
now," Rags said thoughtfully. "A pile of sand; what
kind of a beach is that? There's no sea. What are we
supposed to do?"

"There aren't even any shells," Giangi said mourn-
fully, shaking his head.

"Ready! Shhh! Silence! We're shooting!" For the

umpteenth time the long-haired girl and a young man walked up and down. They walked along a make-believe beach and looked out over a sea that wasn't there.

"Get the children ready!" bellowed the harsh voice. Giangi and Rags jumped down from the boxes and went over to the pretend beach, where there was no sea, no sun, no shells.

Playing wasn't playing anymore.

It had become an unbearable bore. They kept having to start all over again. It seemed that Giangi and Rags had forgotten how to play; anyway that was what all the loud voices hidden behind the huge arc lamps and the camera kept saying. They had to keep repeating the same movements and saying the same words over and over again—five, ten, twenty, a hundred times.

Then, when they were exhausted—they were always having to be repowdered because the sweat was oozing through their makeup—the voice would suddenly, and for no understandable reason, call out, "Good, very good! Perfect! Cut!"

Then they would be left alone for a while. They could gulp cool drinks and put ice on their faces.

They were all taking part in the film, Antonio, Rosalia, Tufty, and Turi also. But Giangi, Rags and Tom were the main characters. They had countless

adventures and had to learn hundreds of lines by heart
—not Tom of course.

Antonio kept thinking of the little pottery by the
side of the lake, where he had worked for all too short
a time. He thought about it and then Maria would
come into his mind and he would suddenly feel calm
and happy.

Revues, television, filming.

It had all happened giddily, out of the blue, in the
space of a few months. One offer led to another; the
agents seemed to go quite mad, and after the group's
first success they fell over each other to sign them up.
Turi took on as many engagements as possible, but
even so he continually had to turn down offers.

As long as it lasts, he said to himself. Then we'll see.
Who knows? They all want us now; they may not
want us later. This sort of thing can't last forever.

Turi did what he thought best with the money they
earned. He thought it best to save. And he saved all
right; he hoarded the money like a squirrel. All he
asked was that the children be patient. He pleaded
especially with Giangi and Rags to be patient. He was
asking them to see this thing through, far from the sea
and the sunshine, to go on pretending to play on a
make-believe beach, their faces covered with makeup
and their eyes swollen from the bright lights, just until
they had all made enough money to live in comfort.

He knew he was asking a great deal, but it was necessary if they were ever again to see Marzamemi, if they were ever again to see the sea, the sand, the shells, the great cushion of seaweed and the delicate chain of coral.

CHAPTER FIVE

Panic

THEY *were* patient.

But patience can be one of the longest things in the world. It can go on forever.

The movie that Turi and the children had made was now showing in all the big towns in Italy. Outside the movie theatres were posters, with Giangi, Rags, and Tom in the foreground and Turi conducting the band in the background.

The film was an enormous success. Good reviews, fan letters, prizes and money, money, money raining into the box offices and into the producers' pockets.

Turi saved up the money that he and the children had worked so hard to earn.

They made two more films. They appeared fre-

quently on television. Giangi and Rags and the ever-present Tom posed for countless publicity pictures.

As part of the publicity for their third movie, the producers planned a grand tour. Giangi and Rags and Tom, all washed and brushed, were to make a tour in a car. But not just an ordinary car.

In front, behind, on the hood and on the doors, the car provided by the producers carried the title of the new film starring the famous Sicilian children, Giangi and Augusto, with their faithful poodle, Tom.

Their plan was to arrive in each town just when most people would be out on the streets. Giangi and Rags had to stand up on the seats of the open car and attract the attention of the crowds.

Every time, wherever they went, the car was recognized, pointed out and usually stopped. People would crowd around the children and ask them for signed photographs.

The producers' staff, which was traveling with the children, would pull out a case stuffed with pictures and distribute them. They pushed pens into Giangi's and Rags' hands and the children would sign their names, very slowly and laboriously, their tongues sticking out with concentration.

"Look how sweet they are. Even the little one can write already!"

"What a clever boy!"

"The dog! Look at the dog! What an intelligent face!"

"Ooooh, aren't they wonderful!" the crowds exclaimed ecstatically.

People who hadn't seen them would get the word from those who had and would run to catch a glimpse and to demand pictures and autographs for themselves.

No one noticed that the children were tired from all the fuss and the traveling, and the excitement. All *they* wanted was to lie down and go to sleep.

Instead, in the evening they had to go to the best movie in town and make a personal appearance. After the film, the scenes of the day would repeat themselves. They had to stand on chairs and the audience would clap madly. They would respond by waving their arms above their heads and blowing kisses. Flashbulbs popped endlessly, newspapers published pictures and articles about the trip. The crowds grew larger and larger, pushing to get a better view, swarming around the child actors, trying to touch them.

One day the throng around Giangi and Rags grew so big that it nearly overturned the car. Rags, with hundreds of hands grabbing at him, fell awkwardly against the rear window and was knocked unconscious. He collapsed into the car. His jacket was in shreds. And Giangi was saved only just in time from the hordes of enthusiastic admirers. Luckily Turi was with them, and he pushed Giangi down into a corner of the car and literally covered him with his own body.

The police pushed forward and tried to clear a path, but the crowd was beside itself. The policemen had to fire into the air.

At this point Giangi burst into tears and frantic, convulsive sobs. He had never quite forgotten those other shots fired long ago; and he seemed to know that once, during the war, someone else, his father or mother, had protected him as he was being protected now.

Turi sensed his terror. He vowed then and there that this meant the end. They couldn't endure any more.

After this episode, Giangi and Rags could not see even a small group of people without feeling an uncontrollable terror. Photographers' flashbulbs made them hysterical. The publicity trip, to which Turi was bound by a contract, ended with the two children trembling and tearful. Turi, once again, said, "Enough!"

The time had come to go back home.

CHAPTER SIX

The End of It All

A LETTER had arrived for Turi. It offered him the post of bandmaster in a little town near Marzamemi.

The difficult contest, with all the trials and tribulations that had followed, had not been enough to bring him what he wanted most in the world. It was the publicity that had done it.

And yet Turi had known how to conduct long before he had appeared on television and in films.

Turi's dream had finally come true; whatever happened, he must take this opportunity.

With the money that Turi turned over to him, Antonio bought the little pottery on the lake. Old Anselmo was tired and ready to retire. When Antonio arrived, Maria was already a young woman and he was a man. One can be a man at sixteen. They had hardly said hello when, as always with her, Antonio felt strangely peaceful and happy. It was as if he had left her only the day before. In fact, strange as it may seem, they had never really been apart.

The surveyor, Giuseppangelo Castronuovo, asked Giuseppangelo Baroni, known as Tufty, if he would like to come and live with him in Palermo. Tufty said yes with such enthusiasm that Castronuovo was deeply moved.

"What do you want to do?" asked Tufty's godfather. He had adopted Tufty officially and would look after him from now on.

"I should like to study," said Giuseppangelo. "I want to be an engineer!"

"Tufty, that cuckoo, going to be an engineer!" Papa Baroni would exclaim from time to time, with tears in his eyes. He could not believe it, especially when he saw the ridiculous faces his son made to amuse his brothers when he and his godfather came to visit.

Rosalia had gone back with Signora Pierina to Number 15 of the street in Milan. The caretaker had deposited Rosalia's share of the money in the bank.

"This must not be touched," she said shortly. "It will do for your dowry when you marry."

Rosalia's mother had died when she was a baby; she was sure that her mother must have looked like Signora Pierina. As Rosalia seemed to have a natural talent for sewing, Signora Pierina enrolled her at a good dressmaking school at her own expense.

"Where there's a will there's a way," she would say firmly to Rosalia.

Turi departed for Marzamemi with the two little boys and the dog. Real sea, shells, sunshine. Everything back to normal. And a real band to conduct.

The Author

Renée Reggiani was born in Milan, Italy. She was graduated from the National Academy of Dramatic Arts and it was her career in the theatre that took her to southern Italy and Sicily. For the first time, she became aware of the poverty and conditions that existed there. From that moment she made the problems of the south her own problems. She began writing stories for young people, turning to that generation "to make them aware of their rights and of their obligations toward their land in a future worthy of the contemporary world."

Mrs. Reggiani is married and lives in Rome. In addition to being an author, she has worked as a journalist, a translator, and in television.

Five Children and a Dog was awarded the National Popular and Scholastic Library Prize in Italy and an honorary diploma presented by the Hans Christian Andersen International Award. It has also been published in England, France, Spain, Germany, Russia, Sweden and South Africa.